OPERATOR 5:
THE SIEGE THAT BROUGHT THE BLACK DEATH

AMERICA'S UNDERCOVER ACE

THE SIEGE THAT BROUGHT THE BLACK DEATH

By Curtis Steele

POPULAR PUBLICATIONS • 2023

CHAPTER 1
A BULLET FOR A BUTCHER

THE AMERICAN flag was still flying over the Post Office Building in New York—headquarters of the American High Command, but Hoboken and Jersey City, directly across the Hudson River, were in the hands of the enemy. The iron battalions of the Purple Emperor, having marched across Pennsylvania, were hammering at the doors of New York, backed up by the huge Purple Fleet which was even now patrolling the coast line from Sandy Hook to Montauk Point.

On the Hoboken waterfront the enemy were moving up a battery of 155 mm guns. They had been unloaded from the ships in the bay, and dragged into position by captive American civilians yoked to the carriages like beasts of burden. Those guns would be able to rake Manhattan Island, once they were in position.

The streets of Hoboken were filled with the lustful, swaggering troopers of the Purple Empire—men recruited from the slums of every city of Europe and Asia, where Rudolph I, Emperor of the Purple Empire, held absolute sway by right of conquest. These troopers, drunk with lust and cruelty, were now indulging in vicious pranks at the expense of the American civilians—both men and women. Their officers gave them a free hand, for it was the custom in the armies of Rudolph to allow the men every degrading excess in the occupied territories.

OPERATOR 5

A group of Purple hussars had swung down a side street, drunkenly singing the vicious "Blood Song" of the Purple Empire. Two of them carried torches to light their way, while the others waved their bayoneted rifles in time to the hideous

THE SIEGE THAT BROUGHT THE BLACK DEATH

Everywhere, the Americans had been checked by the Purple Army!

tune. Suddenly one of them, with the stripes of a corporal on his sleeve, waved his torch, and lunged across the street, shouting exultantly. He had spied an old woman, huddled in the darkness of a ruined building.

The old woman did not attempt to run. She simply stared

vacuously at the lumbering brute. The hussar reached her side, the others following. He shouted to them, "Here's an old cow we can have some fun with!"

He reached out a huge hand, seized the woman by the hair. She uttered a strangled cry as he almost lifted her off her feet with the brutality of his grip. He held her like that for a moment, so that the others could see her face.

One of them exclaimed, "The old witch is blind!"

It was true. The tortured face of the old woman revealed two red splotches where her eyes should have been. She was only one of the many thousands of American women who had been blinded by order of Emperor Rudolph in his ruthless efforts to break the heart of America.*

---

* AUTHOR'S NOTE: It should be noted that the events herein described take place in the twenty-sixth month of the Purple Invasion. Historians have made varied estimates as to the number of American civilians deliberately killed and maimed during those twenty-six months as part of the Purple Empire's cold-blooded policy of terrorization. Stievers places the number at six million. Other authorities have named figures ranging from three to eight million. But the estimate which seems to strike nearest to the truth is that of the Purple historian, Baron Julian Flexner, who was closest to the mad emperor, and in a position to know. He places the figure at no less than *thirteen million.*

Of course, the whole truth will never be known. It is said that twenty thousand men, women and children were driven like cattle over the rim of the Grand Canyon in one afternoon. With such atrocities repeated daily in many places throughout the land, wherever Rudolph's armies marched, it is

THE SIEGE THAT BROUGHT THE BLACK DEATH

The corporal laughed drunkenly. He waved the torch in front of the woman's face. "Can't you see the flame, old woman?" He spoke in a guttural patois that was a mixture of the language of the Purple Empire and of English. These soldiers had picked up a good deal of English in their two years' invasion of the United States, and they were now just barely able to make themselves understood.

The old woman was on her toes, trying to relieve the cruel grip upon her hair. She tried to talk. "Kill me, you brutes. I've been praying for some one to kill me."

The hussars laughed. The corporal twisted his face in a leer. "She wants us to kill her! Ha, ha!"

One of the others suggested, "Push the torch in her face. It's a very good trick."

The corporal nodded. "Good idea!" He raised the torch, prepared to thrust the flaming end of it into the old woman's face. And it was at precisely that moment that a single shot

not surprising that the total should be so high. Neither is it surprising that Americans everywhere fought the invaders with bitter unyielding hate. In fact, Emperor Rudolph's plan to cow America by this show of merciless cruelty only boomeranged against him; instead of breaking the spirit of the defenders, it only increased resistance. This was a trait of American character which the Purple Emperor could never comprehend. He had found these cruel tactics highly successful in Europe and Asia; but he did not realize that the men and women of America still nurtured in their breasts the fierce love of liberty—for which they stood ready to sacrifice all else.

OPERATOR 5

thundered from the darkness at the far end of the street, near the river.

The corporal uttered a high, terrified scream. The torch dropped to the ground, and his fingers relaxed their grip upon his victim's hair. He staggered backward as if an unseen hand had pushed at his chest. Bright red blood spurted out over his tunic. Sound gurgled in his throat wetly, as if mixed with blood. Red foam flecked his lips. His jaw fell slack, his knees buckled, and he crumpled to the ground, falling directly into the searing flame of the very torch he had intended to thrust into the old woman's face.

He was not dead yet, and his body writhed in the fire.

The other hussars suddenly grew quiet, deadly, intent. Their faces reflected grim hate as they spread out, bayoneted carbines thrust forward, and began to run toward that dark portion of the street from which the single shot had come. The old woman also ran, feeling her way along the walls, and disappeared into an alley. But no one watched her. The hussars had forgotten her. They were after bigger game now. Hoboken was occupied by the Purple troops. Purple patrols paraded the streets constantly. Thousands of troops were quartered here, preparing for the scheduled offensive against New York City, across the river. Whoever had fired that shot would find it impossible to escape. And they meant to catch him.

One of the hussars shouted, "There! I see them! Two of them!"

He pointed down the street, toward the river, where two dark, shadowy figures moved swiftly, running. He raised his carbine, fired as he pursued them. The other hussars joined him, hurling a hot hail of lead down the length of the street. Now they were shouting wildly, vindictively. They had sighted their quarry—two fleeing figures.

Answering shouts came from the side streets, mingling with the barking reverberations of the rifle fire. Near-by patrols had heard the shooting, and were closing in. The hunt was on.

Minute after minute, that wild chase continued the fury of the pursuers increasing as their quarry fled like startled deer. They were yelling curses as the race swept on.

CHAPTER 2
FLIGHT FROM FURY

THE TWO fugitives ran silently toward the river, bending low, weaving as they ran. That first hail of lead from the carbines of the hussars had spattered about them harmlessly, for the Purple troopers had fired in haste, without stopping to aim. The two fleeing Americans were approaching the street that bordered the river. They could plainly hear the shouts of the hussars behind them, as well as the heavy sound of padding feet from the riverfront. A patrol was also coming from that direction. Escape was cut off. Shots followed them, gouging the pavement at their feet, whining past their ears. Suddenly, one of the two stumbled, gasped, but recovered and ran on. The other turned, swiftly.

"Diane! Are you hit?"

"It's—nothing, Tim. Keep—going!"

In the darkness, the madly pursuing hussars naturally took those fleeing Americans for two men. But they were mistaken. One of them was a young woman, the other a boy hardly out of his 'teens. Both wore the khaki breeches issued to the American civilians who were drafted for labor battalions by the conquering Purple army; both wore caps pulled low over their heads.

The boy stepped quickly to the side of the girl, put a hand under her arm. He felt wet blood against her coat. "You're wounded, Diane! They got you!"

"It's nothing, Tim. Go on. One of us has to get across the river tonight." She pushed him feebly. "Run—I'll hold them here for a while."

She turned, raising her gun.

The boy, Tim, tightened his lips. "Nix, Diane. I'll not leave you. Come quickly—this way!"

The hussars raised a fierce shout, as they saw one of the two fugitives helping the other toward a dark alley at the side of the street. They held their fire, hoping to capture them alive, and raced forward.

At the same time, the patrol turned into the street from the river. There were now Purple troopers at either end of the street, closing in on the two Americans.

Tim fairly dragged the wounded girl into the alley. Then he stopped, let her rest against the wall, and raised his own gun. He fired back twice at the rushing hussars, then twice more at the patrol approaching from the other direction. His youthful eyes, hard and bleak beyond his years, glinted as he noted that

THE SIEGE THAT BROUGHT THE BLACK DEATH

all four of his shots had taken effect. Both groups of pursuers stopped momentarily as the foremost of their numbers fell to the boy's marksmanship.

Tim, taking advantage of the instant's delay, swung about, threw an arm about the girl, and half-carried, half-dragged her down into the thick blackness of the alley. Behind them, the mad uproar of the blood-thirsty hussars rose in thundering shouts of invective as they closed in on the alley.

Diane gasped, "It's—no good, Tim. I—I can't go—much farther. You've—*got* to leave me."

Tim didn't answer her. He pushed grimly on into the alley, looking behind for the first sign of the hussars, ready to empty his gun at them. He was hugging the wall, virtually supporting Diane.

Now he saw a glimmering light far down at the other end of the narrow alley. There was another street there, and his lips tightened. For that glimmering light was the flare of a torch. Another patrol was turning into the alley at the other end. All escape was blocked off.

In another instant, the pursuing hussars would enter the alley from behind, and that would be the end. There would be only one thing left—to fight in such a way as to make these troopers kill them both. For these Purple butchers had devious and dreadful ways of inflicting lingering and agony-choked death upon those whom they captured alive.

THE BOY kept on, pressing against the wall, eyes darting everywhere desperately in search of some straw of hope. He found that slim promise—with his toe, as he pressed forward.

OPERATOR 5

The bully grabbed the aged, blind woman by the hair!

It was the iron grating of some long-unused cellar. The grating shook under his step.

This part of the city of Hoboken, along the waterfront, had been subjected to severe bombardment in the early days of the Purple Invasion, and many of the buildings were deserted,

THE SIEGE THAT BROUGHT THE BLACK DEATH

abandoned, ready to cave in. Tim could tell that the structure, of which this cellar was a part, must be one such building. The wall was crumbling, decaying. But that loose grating meant temporary respite. The troopers would surely find them down there—eventually. But it would afford them shelter for precious additional minutes. And this boy, though hardly more than fifteen or sixteen, had lived long enough and dangerously enough, to learn that one might transform imminent death into life with the aid of even so little time as an extra minute.*

---

* AUTHOR'S NOTE: Those readers, who are familiar with the events and characters of the Purple Invasion, will already have recognized the boy and the young woman mentioned above as Tim Donovan and Diane Elliot. Though the ponderous tomes which have already been written about the military strategy and the economic and social repercussions of the Purple Wars do not give either of them important mention, such authoritative historians as Harrison Stievers and Baron Julian Flexner have revealed a part of the important roles they played in the defense of America. They were both members of that small but loyally devoted band who operated directly under the orders of the man known as Operator 5. The average run of historians, lacking inside information, have attributed most of their individual exploits to their chief. But Operator 5 himself, in his own notes, not hitherto made available to the public, gives them their full meed of praise. It was Operator 5 who first recognized the possibilities of the ragged newsboy whom he picked up in the slums of New York in the years before the Purple Invasion. It was Operator 5 who taught that boy to shoot, and to ride, to receive and transmit code, to use ju-jitsu, to fight and think like a grown man. Tim Donovan proved a far more able assistant to his chief than might many an

OPERATOR 5

Tim had no time to stop and think, to ponder what might be beneath the grating. Barely a minute had elapsed since they had been sighted by the enemy in the open street. There were, perhaps, ten seconds more before the hussars would be in the alley.

He stooped and pulled at the grating. It came up in his hand. He felt Diane tautening under his supporting arm, and he whispered urgently, "Di, can you jump? There's a cellar here!"

Her eyes were open now. She was forcing them open, biting her lip to hide the pain in her side. She nodded, quickly comprehending. No further word needed to be spoken between these two. They had shared danger often enough together in the past, so that they worked smoothly, like football backs on a gridiron.

Diane gathered her strength, slid to the ground, let her feet dangle over the edge of the dark hole—then dropped. Tim held his breath, waiting to hear her land. Instead of a thud, there was a *splash!*

Water!

Tim's eyes widened. The building was on the riverfront. The bombardment in the early days of the war must have smashed the foundation wall somewhere along the river edge, and the cellar was flooded. There was no telling how high the water was, down in there. Diane, wounded, might not be able to summon enough strength to keep afloat. With pulse beating fast, he slid

---

adult. It is evidence of Operator 5's faith in the boy, that he permitted Tim Donovan to go out on the present mission with Diane Elliot—the nature of which will be revealed in the following pages.

THE SIEGE THAT BROUGHT THE BLACK DEATH

over the edge, pulled the grating back in place over his head, and let himself drop, just as the first thunderous footsteps of the shouting hussars drummed into the alley.

He had shoved the revolver back into his waistband, and now threw his arms out, hoping to deaden the noise of the splash he would make, and hoping, too, that Diane would not be directly beneath him.

She wasn't.

The bitter cold water struck the lad's body like a great slapping gust of wind. His nerves congealed, and he gasped for breath. He struck out, swimming carefully, feeling for Diane, not daring to call to her. The hussars were directly overhead now, stamping about, flinging guttural oaths at each other in their own language. They had met the patrol from the far end of the alley, and realized that their quarry had slipped out of their grasp somewhere along here. They were spreading out now, thrusting their torches high, seeking some doorway in the wall where the fugitives might have escaped. Tim Donovan knew that it would be only a matter of moments before they would find the grating. Even now, the flare of those torches was throwing a glow of light down here into the cellar. The water was soaking his clothes and shoes, making them soggy and heavy, dragging at him. Diane would have that to contend with, in addition to her wound. He must find her quickly, and some means of escaping, or of hiding while the search went on.

HE RAISED his arms, kicked upright, and treaded water, while his eyes darted everywhere in the cellar. The slight illumination, afforded by the torches in the alley, showed him the moldy walls of the cellar, great cracks in the cement. The head of a huge boiler protruded above the level of the water, and he frowned. That boiler must be at least ten feet high, and it was almost submerged.

There was a good deal of noise up above, and he risked a low call. "Diane! Where are you?"

A low rumbling echo of his own voice was the only answer. He waited, treading water, blood pounding in his veins. The echo died away, leaving only the shouted imprecations of the troopers above. He grew panicky. Diane must have hit the water hard. That, together with her wound, might have rendered her unconscious. Perhaps she was at the bottom. He would have to dive for her. How could he resuscitate her, down here in this cellar, with those hussars apt to discover the grating at any moment?

His panic grew. He raised his voice, not caring any more whether or not he was heard by the enemy. *"Di! Di! Can't you hear me?"*

Water dripped from his hair into his eyes, and his wet collar set coldly against his neck. He felt the clinging river clammy against his body. But he was only subconsciously aware of all that. All his senses were alert for the reply he was hoping, praying to get.

Then it came—so faintly that it seemed from miles away.

"Here, Tim. Quick. I'm slipping. I—can't hold on...."

"Where? Where, Di?"

Frantically, his eyes darted into every obscure corner.

"Here...."

And then he saw her.

THE SIEGE THAT BROUGHT THE BLACK DEATH

Her head and shoulders were no more than an obscure blob against the dark bulk of the boiler top, jutting out of the water. She was clinging with one hand to the angle formed by two asbestos-covered steam pipes.

Tim gasped, "Hang on, Di!" Then he struck out toward the boiler.

Overhead, the hussars were tramping violently into every shadowed nook of the alley. They were puzzled, angry. Tim could hear them telling each other that it was impossible for the two Americans to have escaped—that they must be hiding somewhere. And he heard one say, in a loud voice, *"Perhaps in one of the cellars...."*

But he listened with only half an ear. His every faculty was bent upon reaching Diane before she lost her grip upon that pipe. Now he was close to her, and could see her hand slipping. She had no means of renewing her hold, for she could not help herself with her left hand. She was wounded in the left side, and it made it impossible for her to use that arm.

He hadn't been more than ten feet away from her when he heard her call, but it seemed an age to him before he reached her side. He trod water again, and threw one arm around her.

Almost as he touched her, her hand fell away from the pipe, and she emitted a low gasp. It had been the limit of her endurance. She slid into the water, and Tim slipped his arm under her shoulders, endeavored to steady her. Diane was a good swimmer. But she was afraid of losing consciousness in the water. Now, with Tim's arm under her, she struggled to keep her faculties going. She kicked water feebly, breath coming in gasps.

Tim swam with her, around to the far side of the boiler. Here he found a broken steam gauge, and wrapped his fingers around it. It served to keep them afloat without the effort of treading water or swimming. They had reached the far side of the boiler none too soon. For just then there was a scraping sound from above, and some one lifted the grating. A hand thrust a flaming torch down into the cellar, and a thick, guttural voice said, "It is flooded, the cellar."

Another voice called out, "Perhaps they are in there. Perhaps they have dived under the water."

The man with the torch laughed nastily. "Then they can enjoy themselves. We will leave men on guard with torches all through the night. In the morning, we will search every cellar. We will find them, never fear!"

The torch was withdrawn, and the grating replaced. They could hear the troopers walking about above, some one in authority assigning men to guard each end of the alley, and others to patrol its length. They were apparently determined to spare no efforts to catch the two Americans who had shot one of their corporals.

DIANE WHISPERED to Tim, "We're trapped, Tim. I'm too weak to swim. Anyway, there's no place to swim to. In the morning, they'll smoke us out. It's my fault, too. I shouldn't have shot that corporal. But I couldn't help it. I couldn't let him do that to the poor old lady."

THE SIEGE THAT BROUGHT THE BLACK DEATH

Tim said hoarsely, "If you hadn't shot him, I'd have done it, Di. So don't blame yourself. What about that wound? Is it bad?"

"But we had no right to attract attention to ourselves. We—" She broke off, an involuntary groan escaping her. The murky water lapped at her cheeks, spilling into her mouth. A spasm of coughing seized her, and blood from the wound in her side discolored the water.

She still fought against fainting, and Tim exclaimed, "We've got to get away from here!"

But he didn't move. There was no place to go, as Diane had pointed out. He gazed about him desperately in the darkness. Where they floated on the surface of the water, they were some eight feet from the ceiling. He could barely make out two walls of the cellar, one parallel with the alley, and another behind him, at right angles. But this cellar must be an immense place, for he could not even see the other two walls.

But there was some sort of dark bulk across beyond the boiler. It might afford a more secure position than this one. He couldn't hope to hang on to the broken gauge all night. Even if he could, the only thing he might look forward to was discovery and capture by the troopers in the morning.

"Try to float with me, Di," he said. "I'll paddle slowly. There's something over there I want to look at. It's about thirty feet. Do you think you could make it?"

"I'll try."

Her face twisted with pain as she straightened out, succeeded in floating with Tim's arm still under her shoulders. Tim didn't see that grimace of pain in the dark, and he paddled across the thirty feet slowly, laboriously. Two or three times he stopped, as Diane gasped, but each time she managed to say cheerfully, "Go on, Tim. I'm all—right."

At last, they reached the objective. Tim's heart leaped as he realized what it was.

Diane's eyes were closed, and she was breathing fast and trying to keep her face above water. "What—is it, Tim?"

"Di! It's a slanting iron stairway! It goes up to a trapdoor! If we could only make it up there, we'd be on the ground floor of this building!" He maneuvered around the stairway until Diane got a hold on it, then felt with his feet until he found one of the treads under the water. In a moment, they were both standing on it. Slowly, he helped Diane to mount it, until they reached the top, their clothes dripping down into the water beneath them.

Tim pushed upward against the trapdoor. It was not locked, and creaked loudly as he raised it. For a moment, he stood, frozen. If that creak was heard by the troopers outside, they wouldn't wait till morning. They would come after them now.

But there was no sound from the alley.

CHAPTER 3
MISSION FOR A HERO

TIM HELPED Diane up through the trap-door, and she sank down upon the rotting boards of the floor. The

THE SIEGE THAT BROUGHT THE BLACK DEATH

darkness was less intense up here, and Tim could see that they were in an immense, vaulted room. He rubbed the dripping water from his eyes, and looked about him.

There were cobwebs everywhere. High above, the roof of the building was gashed open in two or three places, where shells had smashed through during the bombardment of the early days of the Purple War. These gaping holes afforded glimpses of the star-specked sky. Here and there, in the great room, were huge heaps of debris, where the masonry and beams of the shell-torn roof had fallen. There was a balcony at one end, and another end was entirely open to the night.

Tim knelt beside Diane. "I know where we are, Di. We're in the old ferry building of the Hoboken Ferry! Our own boat is hidden only about a block away!"

Diane shook her head wearily. "I could never make it, Tim. But help me down toward the slip. Maybe we'll find something."

He helped her to her feet, and they managed to make their way down toward the front of the building, facing on the river. Rotting boards almost gave under them, but they got to the ferry slip. An old ferry boat lay at the dock here, with half a dozen wrecked autos still aboard her. That ferry must have been here for two years, caught no doubt, in the first attack of the Purple War. A shell had struck her amidships, smashing the cabin and the wheelhouse, and showering debris upon the cars she was to have carried across the Hudson. The autos must also have been hit, for they appeared to be nothing but twisted hulks of steel.

Diane and Tim had been forced to mount a stairway and cross a sort of bridge that spanned the street, in order to reach the slip. Now they stood here, weighing their chances of escape, while the sounds of passing patrols came to them from the street.

Tim peered down the river. "Our boat's only a block away, Di. If we could get to it—"

"No, Tim. I can't make it. You'll have to go alone."

"If you think I'll leave you, wounded—"

"My wound isn't serious, Tim. I think the bullet nicked one of my ribs. But I feel too—weak to make the boat."

"Well then, I'll stay with you."

"No, Tim. The news we've picked up may mean staving off the destruction of New York. You've got to go across the river and get that news to Jimmy Christopher."

"And leave you here to be captured by those devils? Not—"

"You must, Tim. And I have an idea. I could board that old ferry, and hide on the upper deck. I don't think they'll look there. Then, maybe when you get across with the news, Jimmy can think of some way of getting me off the ferry."

Tim Donovan was doubtful. "Jimmy'd be sore at me for leaving you—"

"You know he wouldn't, Tim. He'd leave me, himself, if it meant as much to the country."

Tim didn't answer for a moment. He knew that Diane was right. Jimmy Christopher, known to the world as Operator 5, would be watching for their return on the other side of the river at just about this time. They had agreed to put out from the Hoboken shore at midnight tonight, whether they succeeded in their job or not.

THE MISSION for which Tim and Diane had volunteered

THE SIEGE THAT BROUGHT THE BLACK DEATH

was one which could best be accomplished by a young woman and a boy, rather than by a man. Any able-bodied man found in the streets of any city in the occupied territory would be immediately conscripted for the labor battalions by the Purple commanders. But a girl and a boy might pass if they were fortunate enough not to be molested by drunken or sadistic troopers.

It was for that reason that Jimmy Christopher had permitted the two to go. The need for a clever, quick-witted scout in Hoboken had been imperative. For eight days now, the Purple Armies had spread their lines about New York, cutting it off almost completely from communication with the rest of the country. One line of communication only had been left open—the sector running from the Hudson out along the Patterson Plank Road. That strip of territory, from the Patterson Plank Road north to the Palisades, and west to Patterson, was heavily entrenched by the Americans, and it was through this route that besieged New York managed to get supplies.

The enemy held all of southern Jersey, and a strong force was in possession of the northern approaches to New York, while the Purple Fleet cut off the city's defenders from all help by sea. But for some strange reason, the Purple Fleet had thus far refrained from bombarding New York. And though the Americans could see the heavy guns being rolled into position on the Jersey shore, no major attack had been launched. There was an ominous quiet in the besieging forces, that bespoke some lurking danger for the defense forces of New York. Tim and Diane had crossed the river, venturing into enemy territory, in search of the reason for that quiet. Though they had not fully pierced the mystery, they had picked up two pieces of news that were vitally important. Tim Donovan knew that the life, either of himself or of Diane Elliot, was not worth the chance of failing to get the news across the river. Therefore, he reluctantly agreed to Diane's plan.

CAUTIOUSLY, THEY worked their way out onto the slip, and climbed aboard the ferry boat. Tim helped Diane up to the upper deck, and stretched her out on one of the long benches there. He opened her coat, and dressed her wound as best he could.

At last, he was finished, and Diane smiled up at him wanly. "Go on, now, Tim. Be careful—don't get caught."

Tim pressed her hand. There was a suspicion of a tear in his youthful eyes. "I'll come back for you, Di."

"I'm sure you will, Tim. But just in case you don't see me again—" she pulled the boy's face down close to hers—"give this to Jimmy for me." She kissed Tim Donovan tenderly.

The boy made his way off the boat almost blindly. Emotion welled in his throat. He wondered if he would be able to face Jimmy Christopher and tell him that he had left Diane here, wounded, and in imminent danger of being captured by the enemy.

That kiss had been intended both for him and for Jimmy Christopher. Diane loved them both, but in different ways. She had fought side by side with Jimmy Christopher throughout the Purple Wars, and long before that. Once an ace newspaper woman, she had virtually given up her career to work with the man she loved, even though she knew that Operator 5 had another mistress who was as dear to him as was she herself.

THE SIEGE THAT BROUGHT THE BLACK DEATH

That other mistress was his country. And as long as his country was in need of him, Diane knew that she came second. Knowing that, she was content. Perhaps, had it been otherwise—had Jimmy Christopher not been that kind of man—Diane Elliot might not have loved him so.

Tim Donovan, who had long served with Operator 5, was intelligent enough to understand that Diane's chances of escaping capture by the enemy were very slim. They would be determined to catch the two Americans who had shot one of their men, and they would persist in the search. They might not think of searching the ferry boat at once, but they would eventually get to it. Moreover, Diane would need medical care, or her wound would become infected.

She must be rescued quickly—that would mean another expedition into Hoboken. Such an expedition would be doubly dangerous, because the enemy would be on the watch in this sector. He, himself, as he made his way among the dark pilings of the wharfs to where his boat was hidden, moved with great care. For the street, less than fifty feet away, was suddenly alive with Purple troopers.

Numerous torches flamed, and men moved about, everywhere. Tim could hear guttural voices uttering crisp commands, and the tread of many feet. He wondered uneasily about this sudden, unusual activity.

He got to the boat undiscovered, and climbed in. It was a small boat, equipped with oars as well as with an outboard motor. The motor could not be used until he was far out in the river, for fear of attracting attention from enemy shore sentries. Diane and he had used this boat to come across in the night before, and had concealed it beneath a rotting, jutting dock only a block from the ferry building. They had been on their way to it when they had seen the corporal torturing that old woman. The old lady's life had been saved—perhaps at the expense of Diane's.

In bitter silence, Tim got into the boat, unshipped the oars, which were wrapped in gunnysack. He sculled carefully out from under the dock, listening to the sounds of the hurrying troopers on the riverfront. His eyes rested broodingly on the decrepit ferry boat where Diane waited, helpless.

Farther up the river, a couple of enemy trawlers lay at their docks. These armed trawlers were equipped with machine guns mounted forward, and a couple of six inch guns on the cabin. They constituted a very definite menace to Tim Donovan now. For if he should be spied from the shore, one of those trawlers could overtake him and shoot him out of the water.

A mile across the river, the shattered skyline of New York City was visible. The breastworks, thrown up along the riverfront by the defending Americans, could be plainly seen. Tim Donovan knew that Operator 5 would be waiting on one of the docks over there, watching through a night glass for him—and for Diane Elliot.

THE SIEGE THAT BROUGHT THE BLACK DEATH

TIM DONOVAN

OPERATOR 5

TIM SIGHED, and got to work upon the oars. He was barely twenty feet from the shore, when he suddenly stiffened and ceased rowing. He, himself, would be barely visible to the soldiers on the shore, for they would be partially blinded by their own torches.

But he was not worried about himself. It was the sharp, commanding voice that he had just heard which turned him cold, and brought the sweat to his forehead.

It was the voice of some high commanding officer who apparently had just arrived, and was now shouting angry commands. The words, spoken in the language of the Purple Empire, came clearly to Tim across the water.

"You fools! Those two Americans must not escape! Throw a cordon of troopers around that ferry building. Bring torches. Bring hundreds of torches. Light up every corner of the building. Search every inch. And search that dock—and that old ferry in the slip. *I want those Americans captured!*"

Tim Donovan could actually feel himself freeze all over as he heard that last command. *They were going to search the jerry boat!*

Wounded as she was, Diane couldn't hope to escape. He recognized the voice of the officer who had issued those orders. It was a certain Colonel Pretorius Salsoun, one of the favorites of Rudolph I, the Purple emperor. He was a heartless beast of a man, huge and beefy in appearance, and endowed with a cunning, virulent mind. The combination of atavistic cruelty and modern cunning had brought Salsoun the appointment of chief of imperial intelligence of the Purple Empire. And the fact that he himself had appeared upon the scene here meant that

THE SIEGE THAT BROUGHT THE BLACK DEATH

he was clever enough to attach more than ordinary importance to the report that two American spies had been discovered on the waterfront.

If he had any suspicion that those two spies were Tim Donovan and Diane Elliot, he would tear the waterfront apart, brick by brick and log by log, to find them. For almost fabulous rewards were offered by the emperor for the capture of Operator 5 or any of his small band of loyal followers.

Now, as Tim Donovan rested on his oars, shivering with the cold of his recent immersion in the cellar, as well as with his icy fear for Diane, he realized that there was no hope of saving Diane Elliot, with Salsoun on the job—unless he thought of some particularly effective ruse to throw the chief of the imperial intelligence off the trail.

But his mind was numb. From where he sat in the skiff, he could see the troopers scurrying about, contingents of them turning into every street and alley in the neighborhood, while others ran out on to the dock where the old ferry boat was tied up. In two or three minutes at the most, Diane would be discovered.

He could see Salsoun, himself, sitting astride a tall black charger, issuing vehement orders left and right, brandishing his long rapier of which he was said to be a master.

Suddenly Tim Donovan's mind clicked into action. His lips tightened, and his hands clenched upon the oars with determination. He was going to make a wild effort to divert attention from Diane—an effort which would almost certainly mean his capture and his failure to communicate his vital information to Operator 5. An older, more experienced agent might not have made such a decision. Indeed, according to all the unwritten rules of espionage, a spy must carry on with his mission, regardless of the fate of his fellow spies in the undertaking. Such is the cold philosophy of that most dangerous and heartless of all occupations—espionage.

But Tim Donovan was very young, very loyal—and impetuous. All his instincts rebelled at rowing away there in the darkness, and leaving Diane Elliot, whom he loved as he would an only sister, to the vindictive mercies of the Purple intelligence chief. So he set about at once to carry out his plan.

WITH TREMBLING fingers, he pulled off his coat. Then he ripped the gunny-sack off the oar-blades, and stuffed the heavy material into the coat. He turned up the coat collar, molded it into a dummy, and set it up in the stern of the boat. In the night it would look just like another person to any one on shore.

Then, with glinting eyes he shipped the oars, slipped aft and kicked over the little outboard motor. His store of gasoline was small, for the fuel was scarce in America these days. Indeed, fuel of any kind was more valuable than the most precious of metals. Two years of destructive warfare had swept America clean of resources, destroying coal mines, oil wells, powerhouses, factories, everything. No city in America had electric light. No auto-

THE SIEGE THAT BROUGHT THE BLACK DEATH

mobiles or planes were now in use except the few for which a precious supply of fuel trickled in through the American lines of communication on the Patterson Plank Road.*

---

* AUTHOR'S NOTE: In the early days of the Purple Invasion, it was the set policy of the Purple General Staff to destroy as they conquered. The Purple armies swept over America from coast to coast, burning, ravaging, pillaging and destroying. The Purple emperor intended, by this method, to impress upon Americans that their country would be a shambles if they resisted; and he hoped that they would yield without fighting rather than see everything that their forefathers had given so much to build, destroyed in a short period. But he misjudged the spirit of America. Americans fought every inch of ground, tooth and nail, rather than surrender the precious right of *liberty* which their forefathers had given so much to gain. Rudolph I, Emperor of the Purple Empire, Master of Europe and Asia, had never met a liberty-loving people like this in all his previous conquests. He could not understand that he was using a method that would not work, so he continued the policy of wholesale destruction. As a result, after two years of warfare, every modern facility for producing the things that the complicated life of civilized man required was destroyed. America was reduced to primitive life, and primitive means of warfare. But whereas the Americans had no means of producing big guns and mighty battleships any longer, Rudolph had at his disposal all the great factories and armament plants of Europe. His ships brought great quantities of the sinews of war to aid his troops. It was the first consignment of this new supply of ammunition which was now to be used against the Americans in the Siege of New York. Operator 5 had, in the last few months, bent every energy to building up once again the great machinery of manufacture which had existed in the United States before the

OPERATOR 5

But there was enough gasoline in the tank to carry him across the river and back. He kicked the motor alive, let it sputter and spark. At the same time, he raised his revolver, and fired it toward the shore. It had not suffered from its immersion, for he kept it in a chamois case under his blouse. Now it exploded hollowly across the water, and the troopers on the shore stopped their hurrying and scurrying to run down to the bank.

They began to point excitedly toward Tim's boat. Tim kept the motor snapping, and headed directly out into the river, angling north to take advantage of the incoming tide. Above the noise of the engine, he could hear the commotion on shore, and hear a stentorian voice shouting, "There they are! They are escaping! After them! Signal the trawler to give chase! Capture them alive, if possible!"

Tim grinned to himself, ruefully. His ruse was working. They were mistaking that gunnysack-stuffed dummy for Diane Elliot. They would give up their search of the docks, and come after him. That was what he wanted. There was little chance of his escaping, however. The trawler would be able to overhaul him before he got halfway across the river. It was his plan to dump

---

Purple Invasion. Some oil wells in Pennsylvania were once more producing, and there were coal mines also in operation, as well as a few factories. But progress was slow, for there were roving armies of Purple troops, under individual war lords owing a loose allegiance to Rudolph, all over the country. And these armies seriously interfered with reconstruction, serving to retard American progress, and to hamstring Operator 5's efforts at checkmating the powerful war machine of the Purple Emperor.

THE SIEGE THAT BROUGHT THE BLACK DEATH

the dummy just before they reached him, pretending that Diane had fallen overboard. Then he would fight it out with the pursuers, shooting until they got him. He would make them kill him rather than be captured alive. He had no wish to be kept in agony for day after day to furnish amusement for the bloodthirsty butchers of the Purple Empire.

He glimpsed the flashes of a semaphore blinking on the shore, and, a moment later, a piercing whistle sounded from the trawler. He heard the creak of its anchor coming up. There was another trawler about a half mile farther up the river, but that one was not stirring. Evidently, they felt that the one boat was enough for the purpose. Those trawlers had been converted into armored war craft by the Purple forces. They were mounted with machine guns, and each had a four-pounder amidships. For some unknown reason, they were the only ships that had entered New York bay. The rest of the immense Purple Fleet had remained, unaccountably, out at sea, patrolling the coast line and landing troops on Long Island and on the Jersey shore.

It was in connection with this queer action of the enemy fleet that Diane and Tim had gone on their spying expedition. The American high command had felt sure that there was something behind the enemy's abstention from entering the bay and sailing up to the very walls of New York. It would have been the obvious thing to do, for there was not a gun heavy enough in the entire city to have offered any serious obstacle to the huge eighteen-inch monsters on board the Purple warships. Tim and Diane had discovered one of the reasons why those ships had remained at sea, and they had also caught a hint of another, and even more disturbing reason. It was this information that Diane considered so vital, that it must be transmitted to Operator 5 even at the cost of leaving her there to be captured by the enemy. **BUT NOW** Tim gave no thought to his mission. His whole attention was wrapped up in carrying out his ruse successfully. In some vague way, he hoped that after he was killed by the armed trawler, which was fast gaining on him, Diane would find some means of escaping from the ferry boat and of getting her information across the river.

He loaded his gun methodically, holding the tiller of the boat firm between his knees. Then he turned and faced into the blinding glare of the spotlight which the swiftly approaching trawler had turned on him. He leaned, as if accidentally, against the dummy in the stern, and sent it hurtling over the side into the water. He heard a shout from the trawler, and saw a machine gunner in the prow turn his gun upon the dummy, saw him send burst after burst into it. They wanted to capture them alive, but they were not taking any chances of one of them escaping by swimming.

Now the trawler closed in swiftly, gaining heavily on Tim's motor boat. They were holding their fire, but the machine gunner in the prow bent over his gun intently, waiting for the order to fire.

Tim crouched near the outboard motor, watching the high prow of the trawler bear down upon him. His face was set grimly. He was waiting for a chance to get the machine gunner. Of course, that would do him no good; there were other guns on that trawler, and other men to man them. But he would go down fighting.

Some one hailed him from the high deck, in English. "You, there! Surrender at once, or we'll blow you out of the water!"

Tim grinned tightly, raised his revolver, and fired at the machine gunner. The man keeled over, and an infuriated voice shouted, "Shoot him!"

Tim emptied his gun at the trawler, then stood up and faced the other ship, waiting for the blast of bullets that would cut him down.

CHAPTER 4
OPERATOR 5 STRIKES BACK

JIMMY CHRISTOPHER, standing at the extreme edge of a pier which jutted out into the Hudson, put down his night glasses with a bitter look in his level blue eyes. For thirty minutes now, he had been watching a certain spot on the Jersey shore across the river—watching for a boat that had not appeared.

He glanced at his wrist watch for the dozenth time, then swung to the two men in army uniforms who stood tensely behind him. "It's twelve-thirty," he said. "Diane and Tim were to put out at midnight, Hank."

He addressed the smaller of the two, a white-haired man whose uniform bore no shoulder straps or other insignia of rank, yet who carried himself with an air of efficient authority which indicated why he had risen to the supreme command of

OPERATOR 5

war-torn America. For this man was Hank Sheridan, formerly the mayor of a small western town, but now Provisional President of the United States.*

Hank Sheridan sighed. His shoulders sagged a bit. His voice was dry, heavy with bitterness. "I can't bear to think of them being captured by Rudolph. He'd have no mercy for them, because he hates you so, Jimmy."

The other uniformed man stirred uncomfortably, then spoke to Jimmy Christopher. "By God, Operator 5, I can't forgive myself for agreeing to let them go. They'll make the fourth to go across the river on this job. The bodies of the first three men to

---

* AUTHOR'S NOTE: Those of our readers who are familiar with the history of the Purple Invasion will recall that when the mighty armies of Rudolph I, Emperor of the Purple Empire, were storming across the Continental Divide in the first ruthless wave of invasion, it was Hank Sheridan who mustered the men of his town, armed with rusty muskets and miscellaneous weapons, to meet that vicious horde. Subsequently, he was given command of a division of the American Defense Force. And when a ravaged America finally succeeded in stemming the victorious march of the Purple Armies, it was in no small measure due to the brilliant leadership of Hank Sheridan. Thus, it was little wonder that when the Second Continental Congress met at Chicago, they should choose him as Provisional President And now that the Purple hordes were once more rallying to the attack of America's key city, Hank Sheridan had come in from Michigan where he had been trying to reassemble a Continental Congress dispersed by the enemy. He had stolen into New York through the Purple lines the previous night for the purpose of joining the defenders of the city in their last stand.

THE SIEGE THAT BROUGHT THE BLACK DEATH

try it have been floated back to us, each time, with the tide. And God—the things those Purple swine did to them. Now we'll get the bodies of Diane Elliot and Tim Donovan—that way!"

This man was General Sylvester Ferrara, commander of the Twenty-seventh route army, hastily moved into New York to hold it against the Purple divisions. Ferrara had risen in a short time from an inconspicuous lieutenancy to this responsible post, because of sheer ability and devotion to duty. He was an excellent soldier. And he was wholeheartedly devoted to Diane Elliot and Tim, as well as to Operator 5.*

---

* AUTHOR'S NOTE: Of course every American knows that General Ferrara later rose to the Presidency of the United States. What few people are aware of, however, is the fact that Ferrara's success was all due to a chance meeting one day, between himself and Operator 5. It was in the heat of battle, when an emergency arose, and Ferrara, then only a young lieutenant, was the only officer available who could assist Jimmy Christopher in a ticklish piece of business. Lieutenant Ferrara acquitted himself so well, that Operator 5 recommended him for advancement. After that, he distinguished himself time after time, rising to every emergency, until he was made commander of the Twenty-seventh route army by popular proclamation of the troops. Of course, a man of his ability might have attained success without the element of chance, and without the recommendation of Operator 5. But Ferrara was never the man to deny credit where credit was due. And he never forgot the first boost that Jimmy Christopher had given him. There came a time, in the not-too-distant future, when he had occasion to repay Operator 5 amply for anything Jimmy had done for him—but at the risk of his life. Ferrara did not hesitate. That incident, throwing an interesting sidelight on the character of

OPERATOR 5

Jimmy Christopher said tonelessly, "Don't blame yourself, Sylvester. When Diane makes up her mind to a thing, nobody can stop her. And Tim's pretty much the same way. I've never been able to keep that kid out of danger. He always pokes his nose in."

General Ferrara motioned to a boat that was riding alongside the dock, with her nose pointed out toward the river. "I've ordered this old police boat to stand by in case of emergency. It was the fastest boat of the New York Police Department in the old days when I pounded a beat, before the Purple Invasion. It's equipped with two machine guns. If anything should turn up, you can count on—"

He broke off as Jimmy Christopher, who had raised the night glasses to his eyes once more, tensed and uttered a sharp exclamation.

Hank Sheridan pushed up close to him, with Ferrara on the other side.

"What is it, Jimmy?" Sheridan demanded. This old man, upon whose shoulders sat a greater responsibility that had ever burdened any President of the United States, yet found time to be genuinely concerned about two people whom he loved very much. "Do you see anything?"

Operator 5 swore softly under his breath. "That's a boat

---

a great man, will be related in these chronicles at another time, in its proper place. For details of the first meeting of these two, the reader is referred to "The Bloody Frontiers."

THE SIEGE THAT BROUGHT THE BLACK DEATH

putting out from the Hoboken shore! It's the spot we've been watching!"

The other two were silent, taut, while Jimmy kept the glass glued to his eye. "It's Tim, all right! And he's doing something damned funny. He's taken off his coat, and is stuffing it with the gunnysacks from his oars. He's alone. Diane—God, Diane's not with him!"

While Jimmy Christopher continued to watch, General Ferrara, who thought quickly in emergencies as a good soldier should, ran to the edge of the dock and called down to the skipper of the ex-police boat, "Turn over your engine. Be ready to throw off the line and pull out!"

The crew of the police boat burst into activity.

In the meantime, Jimmy watched through his glass. "That damned kid!" he said to Sheridan and Ferrara. "He's started up his outboard motor, and he's gunning it. You'd think he *wanted* to attract the enemy's attention to himself! And now—*good God, he's shooting at the shore!*"

"He's crazy!" President Sheridan snorted. "What—"

Jimmy Christopher was already running toward the police boat. "Not Tim!" he shouted back to Sheridan. "Tim's got an idea, or he wouldn't be doing a thing like that. I think I can guess what the idea is!"

He landed on the deck of the police boat in a running leap from the dock, and the skipper threw in the clutch. The boat darted away from the dock like a projectile, heading out across the river directly toward Tim's boat.

OPERATOR 5, tight-lipped, took the helm from the man

OPERATOR 5

at the wheel, and held it in a straight line for his objective, not bothering about current. His quick eyes had already spotted the armed trawler putting out from the Jersey shore after the boy. His eyes grew bleak. He would reach Tim at about the same time as the trawler. But how to keep the trawler from shooting Tim out of the water?

The police boat was making thirty knots now—at least twice the speed of the trawler. But it wasn't fast enough for Operator 5.

"Haven't you got any more speed?" he demanded of the skipper, shouting to make himself heard above the screaming of the wind.

The skipper shook his head. "I'm giving it all she'll take now," he shouted back.

They were bearing down upon the motor boat, and Tim's back was to them. So absorbed was the boy in firing at the trawler, that he did not seem to hear the approach of the police boat. His back was to them. Jimmy wanted to shout at him—not to fight but to run for it. It would have been useless.

Operator 5 swung his helm to starboard, cutting a course that would head him directly for the trawler instead of for Tim's boat. He shouted to the crew, "Prepare to lower the life boats. I'm going to ram that trawler!"

A low cheer of encouragement rose from the men, and they ran to the davits, loosening the lines holding the life boats, of which there were two. They understood what Jimmy Christopher had to do. Their own two machine guns would be at a disadvantage against the four-pounder mounted on the cabin of the trawler. Even by opening up with their guns, they could

THE SIEGE THAT BROUGHT THE BLACK DEATH

not prevent the enemy from shooting down Tim Donovan in his unprotected boat.

But the iron prow of the police boat, used for battering down burning abutments when there was a fire on the waterfront, made an excellent battering-ram.

Now they were close behind Tim's little craft, and Jimmy Christopher was steering a course that would carry him past Tim, head on against the trawler. Tim was still unaware of their approach.

Operator 5 saw him rise, level his revolver at the trawler, and then stand there, shoulders back, awaiting the death blast. Jimmy could spare the lad only a quick side glance, and his eyes flickered with admiration for the boy's courage.

"Good kid!" he muttered.

Then he had no time for anything but the matter in hand. The crew of the trawler had run to the rail to send a hail of musket fire at the police boat, while their captain maneuvered so that the four-pounder would bear on the Americans. They had expected that the American boat would come up close, deliver a volley, then veer off. It never occurred to them that the crazy Yankees would ram them—until too late.

Cries of sudden fear burst from the enemy boat. The machine gunner, who had been training his weapon on Tim's boat, abruptly sprang up and ran to the farther rail as he realized what Jimmy Christopher intended to do. The captain of the trawler screamed at him to veer off. The crew scattered from the rail, running in every direction, impelled by uncontrollable panic.

OPERATOR 5

Now Tim Donovan saw the police boat for the first time. His voice rose in a yell of appreciation. "Attaboy, Jimmy—"

The rest of his shout was drowned in the rumbling thunder of the impact of the police boat against the trawler. The iron prow of Jimmy's boat cut through the wooden hull of the trawler like a cleaver slicing through a rotten log. Boards splintered and wrenched, groaned and tore.

Operator 5 swung his helm hard, and shouted, *"Full speed astern!"*

The skipper reversed his engines, and the powerful propeller of the police boat churned up great geysers of water as it backwashed, dragging the craft astern. There was another great rending noise, and the police boat dragged itself clear of the trawler, its smooth sleek prow sliding out and leaving a huge raw wound in the trawler's side.

The river rushed into the space the prow had opened for it, and the trawler listed to port with appalling suddenness. One or two of her crew jumped, but the others were too stunned to move. An instant later, it was all over. The enemy ship seemed to be sucked down into the river, as if dragged inexorably by a thousand undersea hands. It shot downward, leaving a great round saucer of suction that dragged the crew with it, together with the two men who had jumped but had not been able to swim clear of the wreck.

The police boat kept churning astern, and Jimmy Christopher had thrown a line overside, which Tim Donovan caught. The boy braced himself in the boat, winding the hawser twice around his body. In this manner, he was towed safety out of the

THE SIEGE THAT BROUGHT THE BLACK DEATH

suction belt caused by the sinking trawler. Now Jimmy Christopher raised a hand, and the skipper swung the engine lever to neutral. With a great shivering sigh, the police boat came to rest in the middle of the river, and a dozen willing hands helped Tim Donovan aboard.

He was expelling his breath in lusty gusts, and when Jimmy Christopher came running down the deck to him, the boy could barely catch enough breath to greet him.

Operator 5 clapped him on the back. "You've made it, Timmy! That was pretty close!"

THE CREW of the police boat were cheering wildly, while hundreds of Purple troopers on the Jersey shore were dancing up and down the river bank in ineffectual rage.

The skipper came over, and Tim Donovan shook hands with him. "Thanks, mister—"

"Don't thank me." The skipper grinned. "Thank Operator 5 for his quick thinking. It was his idea to ram the ship. I'd clean forgot we have an iron prow. And it did us no damage, either. We haven't even sprung a leak. Didn't have to use the life boats."

Tim Donovan grinned back at him. "We have met the enemy, and they are ours!" he quoted.

Jimmy Christopher nodded seriously. "Rather, they are Davey Jones's. But what was the idea of starting your motor so close to the shore, Tim—and where's Diane?"

Immediately, Tim grew solemn. "Gosh, Jimmy, Diane's wounded. Not bad, but she couldn't make it to the boat. She's in that old ferry boat over there, and they were going to search

OPERATOR 5

THE SIEGE THAT BROUGHT THE BLACK DEATH

Squarely into the enemy trawler,
Operator 5 rammed the police boat!

OPERATOR 5

it, so I rigged up the dummy to make the enemy think we had both got away in the boat."

"I see," Jimmy said thoughtfully. "You were going to let them kill you, so they'd stop looking for Diane."

"Aw—" Tim ground his toe in the planking of the deck, flushing—"I just didn't think about it. I did it."

The skipper interrupted. "What'll we do now, Operator 5? The enemy are wheeling a couple of six-inch guns down to the riverfront. I guess they figure on blowing us out of the water. And that trawler up the river has steam up. They'll be after us with their four-pounder. Will we go back?"

Jimmy Christopher looked longingly at the ferry boat where he knew Diane was lying, wounded. She needed medical attention, needed to have that wound dressed to prevent infection. She might still be discovered and captured in spite of Tim Donovan's trick. Operator 5 would have liked to make a quick stab at rescuing her off the ferry. But it was a fool-hardy thing to try, and he had no right to risk the lives of the crew of the police boat in such a suicidal attempt. He saw that Tim was watching him expectantly, hoping he would decide to beard the whole enemy garrison of Hoboken in an attempt to snatch Diane out of there. But he shook his head. Reluctantly, he told the skipper to make back to the New York side of the river.

"It won't do, Tim," he said. "The chances are a thousand to one against our getting Diane off there, and, if we failed, the enemy would guess what we'd been trying to do, and would find her there. We'd only be giving her away if we tried and failed. I

THE SIEGE THAT BROUGHT THE BLACK DEATH

think we'll make a little trip to Hoboken ourselves, later on in the night—maybe just you and I, eh?" He nodded.

"That's swell, Jimmy!" Tim beamed. "And now let me tell you the news that Diane and I picked up—"

"Save it. You can tell it to Hank Sheridan and General Ferrara when we get back to shore. Now you just lie down there and take it easy."

Tim obeyed. He needed a little rest after the experience he had just been through. How badly he needed the rest he didn't know until he lay down. In spite of his pounding heart, the peril and excitement of the last couple of hours, he fell off to sleep at once.

When they reached shore, just ahead of the first shells from the six-inch guns on the Jersey side, he was still sleeping with the soundness of youth. Jimmy Christopher picked him up tenderly in his arms and carried him up on the dock, where Hank Sheridan and Sylvester Ferrara had been waiting, restraining their impatience with difficulty.

CHAPTER 5
THE SECRET OF THE SIEGE

TWENTY MINUTES later, Tim Donovan was telling his story in the Post Office Building, to the officers of the American Defense Force. "There's something big in the wind, all right," the boy told them. "The Purple Empire is planning a knockout blow for us. But just what it's going to be, I don't know. When Diane and I landed in Hoboken last night, we separated,

OPERATOR 5

and I went and hung around the officers' mess at Purple G.H.Q. They're using civilian prisoners there for dishwashing and cleaning, and I let the commissary sergeant see me. He grabbed me, and put me to work as bus boy. They didn't think I understood a word of the Purple language, so they were pretty free with their talk while I was around the table.

"Well, I was picking the dishes from the table where this Colonel Salsoun sat with a couple of high ranking officers, and they were talking about something that's planned to take place on Wednesday. That makes it tomorrow. I heard Salsoun laugh, and say to the others that that would be the end of New York City, and that the Americans wouldn't have any more fight left in them after Wednesday."

As the boy finished, the officers glanced worriedly from one to another. Hank Sheridan, who presided at the long council table, scratched his head perplexedly. "And you don't know anything more than that about the plan?"

"Only this," said Tim. "I heard one of the other officers tell Colonel Salsoun that it was pretty clever to be able to destroy a whole city with a loss of only a hundred men."

"A hundred men?" General Ferrara looked perplexed. "I don't see how they could do it, I've got thirty thousand men here. There are another fifteen thousand in Westchester County, entrenched around the Kensico Reservoir, to protect our water supply. And there are at least ten thousand more out on Long Island, without counting Reilly's Fifth Connecticut Militia, who crossed the Sound into Long Island yesterday under the noses of the enemy blockade. Then there are more than forty

THE SIEGE THAT BROUGHT THE BLACK DEATH

thousand men in Jersey, protecting our lines of communication with Pennsylvania. I don't see how a hundred men—"

Jimmy Christopher interrupted him. "You can be sure, Sylvester, that it's some devilish sort of plot that will take us by surprise. But at least we are forewarned to some extent. We can be on our guard." He turned to Tim. "Go on, Timmy. You said there was something else you had learned."

The boy nodded. "It was Diane who found this out. While I worked the officers' mess, she went out to the home of a girl, she knew who's married and living in the Occupied Territory. She talked to a lot of civilians, and she got one piece of news. The Purple Fleet can't move in on New York because—believe it or not—there's not a pilot on any of the boats that knows the harbor well enough to bring in a heavy ship!"

General Ferrara chuckled. "They can thank Operator 5 for that. It was his idea to tow away the Ambrose lightship, and to remove the buoys that marked the navigation channel. Only a pilot who's been brought up in New York bay could guide a battleship into harbor."

Hank Sheridan nodded. "That's right. But don't forget that the light destroyers could make it, if they worked their way in slowly, and took frequent soundings."

Tim Donovan smiled. "Anyway, Diane found out that Emperor Rudolph is offering a hundred pounds of pure gold, a commission in the Purple Navy, and immunity for the whole family of any American pilot who will volunteer to bring in their big battleships. They could go to work, of course, and mark out the channel—but it seems to be a matter of time. For some

OPERATOR 5

reason, they want to get their ships up the Hudson past New York."

General Ferrara nodded. "I can see that. They want to contact General Shan Hi Mung's Mongol Army, which is marching around from the northwest. If they can supply Shan Hi Mung with munitions and big guns, the Mongol Army can sweep down on New York from the north, and overwhelm our forces in Westchester County."*

---

* AUTHOR'S NOTE: It will be recalled that the Mongol war lord, Shan Hi Mung, was at one time one of the leading generals of the Purple Empire, having command of the huge contingent of Mongol warriors, fighting under their own banner, but owing allegiance to Rudolph I. But later, it was Shan Hi Mung who betrayed his master, and who made the Purple emperor a nominal prisoner, holding him until he had promised to permit Shan Hi Mung to become Emperor of America—if and when he could subdue it. The historic document wherein Shan Hi Mung and Rudolph agreed to this disposition of America, is now in the possession of the American Museum of History. It sets forth that Shan Hi Mung and all his descendants shall forever owe fealty to Emperor Rudolph I, but that they shall enjoy full suzerainty over America; that they shall pay to Emperor Rudolph or his descendants an annual tithe of twenty thousands pounds of gold and forty thousand slaves recruited from among the American civilian population; and that they shall at all times aid the Purple emperor in any war of offense or defense. There are many other interesting paragraphs in this document, and it would repay study by any one who is interested in the greed and rapacity of human beings. It was this General Shan Hi Mung who had almost succeeded in marching unopposed to New York City, but who had been stopped at Valley Forge by

THE SIEGE THAT BROUGHT THE BLACK DEATH

THE VARIOUS officers seated around the table began a heated conversation, each advancing some theory of his own as to the nature of the *coup* which the Purple Armies were planning for Wednesday.

General Ferrara raised a hand for silence. "Gentlemen," he said solemnly, "there is one thing we must bear in mind. *The Purple Fleet must not pass up the Hudson.*" He paused a moment, then went on. "I have every available gun mounted along the river to bear on the lightships of the Purple Fleet, if they should enter the river. I think we could stop any destroyers, or even light cruisers. But if the ships of the line—the big dreadnoughts—get past the channel, my guns wouldn't be any good at all against those eighteen-inch guns they mount. They could sail right past us, and turn their barrage on our troops holding the Patterson Plank Road. Once they dislodged them, our supply lines would be shut, and we'd starve to death. This is a big city. We have over three million civilians in addition to our troops. We haven't got enough food stored to last us more than a week. So you see how important it is to keep the heavy ships out of the river!"

Operator 5 and five thousand brave American volunteers. After the Battle of Valley Forge, Shan Hi Mung had retreated and encircled the American army, marching around by a long and circuitous route, pillaging and burning on the way, until now he was advancing upon New York from the north simultaneously with the advance of Rudolph's newly recruited Purple troops from the west, and of the Fleet from the ocean. Thus, New York City was encircled by a ring of steel, and virtually cut off from the rest of the country, except for that life line along the Patterson Plank Road.

OPERATOR 5

The officers around the table agreed with him, and many offered suggestions as to how to insure the maintenance of the communications line. In the midst of this discussion, Hank Sheridan rose, and motioned to Jimmy Christopher to come with him. He led him to a corner of the conference-room, and faced him, eying him keenly.

"Your mind isn't on all this right now, is it, Jimmy?"

Operator 5 nodded, his lips tight. "That's right, Hank. I'm thinking of Diane over there in that ferry boat—wondering if gangrene hasn't set in in that wound of hers."

Sheridan put a hand on his shoulder. "All right, Jimmy. Forget about all this. Ferrara is a good man, and he has a good general staff. They'll handle the routine situation here. You get out and figure a way to haul Diane back here." He paused, then added quickly, "And maybe while you're doing it, you'll get a line on just what the Purple high command is planning for us for tomorrow. That's what has me worried."

Operator 5's eyes narrowed. "There may be nothing to it. And yet—that Salsoun is a clever fellow. I'll do my best, Hank."*

---

* AUTHOR'S NOTE: I have been severely criticized of late, by a number of people who have complained that I have not adhered to the truth, and that I have put words into the mouth of Operator 5 which he never uttered. These people have no doubt been reading Actionized versions of the events of the Purple Wars. The authors of these Actionized versions have caused Operator 5 to speak in a different manner from that shown in these chronicles. At least, that is the impression I gather, for my critics have recently taken exception to the way that Jimmy Christopher talks to Hank Sheridan. They

THE SIEGE THAT BROUGHT THE BLACK DEATH

Sheridan's shrewd old eyes were fixed on him. "Now, remember, Jimmy, I don't want you taking any wild chances. We need you badly—can't afford to lose you. Have you got a plan?"

Jimmy Christopher nodded. "I've just been working something out—since hearing from Tim that the Purple Navy is looking for a pilot. I'll want to use that Purple Navy launch that ran aground the other day in the Kill van Kull. We captured the entire crew with its officers, didn't we?"

"Yes. The launch is in the dock at Spuyten Duyvil, and the officers and crew are in the detention camp. We confiscated their uniforms and papers, as you suggested, and they're all intact."

"Good. Will you heliograph up to the dock at Spuyten Duyvil, and ask them to put a crew on the launch and bring it

---

say that Operator 5 would never address the President of the United States of America in such a way as I have indicated in these accounts; that he would not presume to call him by his first name. And they further criticize me for referring to the President, as I often do, as "Sheridan." These critics feel that Harrison Sheridan, First Provisional President of the Second Republic of the United States of America, has become more or less of a symbol to be revered, like George Washington, the first President of the First Republic. My reply to these critics is that I am dealing not with the Harrison Sheridan whom they revere from the respective of history, but with the living, human man of that very day—the real Hank Sheridan. Let it also be borne in mind that a good deal of painstaking work has gone into the reconstruction of these chronicles from the very notes written almost on the scene of action, by Operator 5, by Diane Elliot, and later by Tim Donovan. And if my critics can point to a more authoritative source, I shall be glad to have them do so.

OPERATOR 5

down? I'll want fifteen seamen as volunteers to go along with me, dressed in the enemy naval uniforms. I'll want all the officers' papers. I'd also like to get two good Annapolis graduates, if there are any in New York, to put on the uniform of the Purple junior officers."

Sheridan took a pad of paper from his pocket and scribbled an order to the Spuyten Duyvil dock superintendent. He handed it to an orderly, with instructions to heliograph in code at once.

"The Purple intelligence doesn't know yet that we've captured that launch," he told Operator 5. "They think it's still patrolling the upper Hudson. That'll be in your favor. Now—what's your plan?"

"It's not really a plan, Hank. It's a shot in the dark. I'll impersonate the commander of that launch, and put into Hoboken. I'll mingle with the officers there, and see what I can learn about tomorrow's plan. And when I leave—I'll take Diane!"

Hank Sheridan whistled. "It's bold, Jimmy—too bold for you to get away with—and virtually impossible. But I wish you luck—and that I could be going along." He pressed Jimmy's hand.

Operator 5 turned to go. He saw Tim Donovan eying him from the conference table, where the boy had been listening to the discussion of the general staff—a thing no boy of fifteen had ever been privileged to do before. Tim was about to get up and join Jimmy, but Operator 5 said swiftly to Sheridan, "Keep Tim here, Hank. He's had enough for one night already."

Then he slipped out of the door before Tim Donovan could reach him.

THE SIEGE THAT BROUGHT THE BLACK DEATH

CHAPTER 6
TO HOBOKEN—OR HELL

THREE HOURS later, a trim, well-scrubbed Purple Navy launch nosed its way into a dock in Hoboken. By a strange coincidence, this dock was only a hundred feet or so from the old ferry slip where Diane Elliot lay wounded. The crew of fifteen men appeared efficient and well-trained. Even though in Purple territory, the crews of the launch's two machine guns did not leave their posts. The lookout in the bow remained on watch.

The commander of the launch, a certain Captain von Grosse, as his papers showed, came ashore with a detail of ten men behind him. He was attired in full uniform, with a long rapier at his side, and several strings of gold braid across his uniform, indicating that in addition to his rank of naval captain, he was also a count of the Purple Empire, and as such entitled to the respect of all officers, even those superseding him in rank.

The sailors who marched behind him were all armed with the short clubs with which Purple seamen were provided when on shore leave in Occupied Territory. All seemed taut, alert, in sharp contrast to the easy indifference of their captain. Many of them cast surreptitious glances toward the old ferry slip.

A sub-lieutenant of land marines of the Purple Empire was at the dock with a detail of men to meet the captain, word having been flashed to the commandant's quarters that the launch was approaching. The sub-lieutenant was very obsequious when he saw the braid of nobility upon the broad chest of the naval captain, who showed him his credentials with an easy good nature, and the lieutenant was thoroughly satisfied, never doubting the authenticity of this man.

Operator 5 had little fear that any one here would know the real von Grosse, whom he was impersonating. For he had taken care to look up von Grosse's history, and had learned that the captain was one of those who had just come over from Europe with the latest additions to the Purple Fleet. Jimmy had changed his appearance a little, by giving his complexion a slight swarthy hue, and by broadening his nose with tiny aluminum plates in the nostrils. Also, he had thickened his eyebrows so that they appeared quite bushy.

Many soldiers of the Purple Empire knew Operator 5's face, for his picture was published on hundreds of thousands of hand-bills, offering fabulous rewards for his capture. But no one would look for Operator 5 in the person of this aristocratic, haughty naval captain, who had just landed from a navy launch.

The sub-lieutenant saluted respectfully, and asked Captain von Grosse if there was anything he could do for him, and whether he had come on official or private business.

Captain von Grosse shrugged. "It is of a semi-private nature. I would appreciate it very much if you could tell me where to find the Herr Colonel Salsoun, of the Imperial intelligence."

Jimmy Christopher spoke the language of the Purple Empire flawlessly, as he did nine other languages. His accent was even more authentic than that of the young lieutenant.

"I shall be glad to oblige you, Herr Captain," the officer replied. "It so happens that I saw him only fifteen minutes ago,

THE SIEGE THAT BROUGHT THE BLACK DEATH

in the public room of the Empire Restaurant, hardly two blocks from here. I will escort you there."

Operator 5's disguised seamen fell in behind him, joining the sub-lieutenant's detail. The men exchanged news, Jimmy's boys inventing news of the fleet for the benefit of the lieutenant's hussars.

Hank Sheridan had been careful to find volunteers for this undertaking who spoke the Purple language fluently, and they were able to carry on a flow of conversation and banter which raised no suspicions.

Jimmy, himself, tried to feel out the lieutenant. "My visit here," he said, trying to sound mysterious, "has to do with that which is to take place tomorrow."

The other raised his eyebrows knowingly. "Ah, yes—Colonel Salsoun's brilliant plan. You know what it is?"

Jimmy's face was inscrutable. "Would I be here otherwise?"

"I see. Then you must be of those in the navy who are to take part in it. They say there are only four men who really know the nature of the plan—the emperor, the commandant, Colonel Salsoun, and the naval officer who is to carry it out. Colonel Salsoun is expecting a naval officer to receive instructions. No doubt you are that officer."

"No doubt." Jimmy's blood was racing. If he could carry off this impersonation successfully! But there was little chance of fooling the wily Salsoun that far. However, it would be worth a try.

THE EMPIRE RESTAURANT had formerly been McGuire's Grill. The invaders had renamed it, driven out all

OPERATOR 5

THE SIEGE THAT BROUGHT THE BLACK DEATH

Sword out, Jimmy leaped forward
to meet Salsoun's blade!

civilians and converted it to the use and entertainment of the Purple officers. The sub-lieutenant escorted Jimmy inside, and led him to a table where a huge, beefy man sat, talking to a nervous and frightened girl.

The beefy man wore the uniform of a colonel of intelligence, and the sub-lieutenant, saluting respectfully, introduced Captain Count von Grosse to him. "This, Captain von Grosse, is Colonel Salsoun."

Salsoun had no suspicions of the young nobleman who was being introduced to him. In fact, he nodded in satisfaction. "I see," he said, "that Admiral von der Selz has sent me a new man. You have recently arrived from Europe?"

"I have only been in charge of my launch since today," Jimmy answered him truthfully. "It shall be a great privilege for me to assist the famous Colonel Salsoun."

The colonel's thick lips wreathed in a smile at the flattery. He waved the girl away from the table. "I want her held here," he instructed the lieutenant. "I shall need her in a few minutes."

He motioned Jimmy Christopher to take a seat. His eyes strayed to the other end of the room, where Jimmy's seamen had spread out at tables, and were ordering beer. "You have brought your men along, I see."

"Only a few of them," Jimmy told him.

He, himself, also cast a quick glance about the barroom. It was a large place, with a long bar at one end. There were some twenty Purple hussars, with their high black shakos, lounging at one end, but not drinking. These, Jimmy understood, were the personal guard of Colonel Salsoun. In addition, there were

THE SIEGE THAT BROUGHT THE BLACK DEATH

thirty or forty officers of various ranks, drinking at the tables, and making themselves unpleasant to the young American girls waiting on the tables. These girls were compelled to serve the officers in the various barrooms and restaurants in the Occupied Territory, under pain of having their families executed, and of suffering worse, themselves.

Jimmy felt his blood boil at sight of some of the indignities that were offered to these young women, as they served the officers. But he managed to contain himself under Salsoun's scrutiny.

Salsoun said to him, "Are all preparations made aboard the destroyer that is to be used for tomorrow's plan?"

Jimmy saw that the colonel was watching him carefully. Did the Colonel suspect him at all, and was he laying a trap with an artful question?

Jimmy replied, "All your instructions have been carried out to the letter thus far, my Colonel."

Salsoun grunted. "That is good. You have the two big cages erected on the deck? I hope they are strong. They will need to be strong." He chuckled. "No doubt, Admiral von der Selz, and yourself, are wondering as to the nature of this plan of mine?"

Jimmy forced a smile. "I am *very* curious, my Colonel."

Salsoun clucked. "You will have to contain your curiosity. I will not reveal the plan until one hour before its scheduled time. Admiral von der Selz has the sealed envelope of instructions. You will return to the flagship, and there he will open the envelope and give you your orders."

"But, sir, I thought that you wanted to give me the particulars now—"

"Not at all, Count von Grosse. I merely wanted to meet the man whom von der Selz selected to carry it out—" he leaned forward, emphasizing the next words—*"so that the emperor and I would know whom to punish if the plan goes wrong!"* Jimmy Christopher's lips tightened. "Do not worry yourself, my Colonel. From this moment on, my every attention shall be focused upon your plan!"

Salsoun nodded in satisfaction. The double meaning in Jimmy's words was lost upon him. "That is well. Now as to a pilot. You will need a pilot through the harbor. I understand there is none in the fleet capable of picking his way since the damned Americans destroyed the Ambrose Lightship, and removed the buoys from the ship channel."

"That is true, my Colonel."

"Well, *I* am going to get you a pilot. That girl—" he motioned toward the frightened girl to whom he had been talking when Jimmy entered—"is Daisy Gait, the granddaughter of an American pilot named John Gait. It is said that he knows every ripple of water in the upper and lower bay, and that he could guide a ship into harbor with his eyes blindfolded. He is our prisoner, and is being brought here now. I shall ask him to pilot your destroyer."

"But," Jimmy asked, "will this American agree?"

Salsoun laughed nastily. "He will agree. I have a way of making people agree!"

OPERATOR 5 cast a quick glance at the girl. She was only

THE SIEGE THAT BROUGHT THE BLACK DEATH

about eighteen or nineteen, slight of build, with dark bobbed hair and a little mouth that was tight now with the same fear which was reflected in her eyes. The two hussars were holding her none too gently and Jimmy could see her young breasts heave with emotion.

The great room of the restaurant was noisy, boisterous with the crude, unrestrained jokes of the Purple officers. At a near-by table, lieutenants were amusing themselves by sticking out their feet to trip the young waitresses who went past them bearing trays.

Salsoun laughed, "It is very fortunate that we discovered this girl to be the granddaughter of John Gait. We knew he was in Hoboken, but we could not locate him. When we posted a notice that this girl was in our hands, he came in to the commandant's office and surrendered himself, as we had demanded in the notice. You see, we promised to spare her, if he would give himself up."

"And you intend to keep that promise, Herr Colonel?" Jimmy asked.

Colonel Salsoun winked in reply. "Only so far, Captain. Gait will have to pilot your destroyer for you, or we will—do things to her!" He laughed harshly now.

Just then the door opened, and a corporal and one hussar entered, with John Gait between them. Gait was a white-haired, white-bearded man, who clattered into the room on one good leg and one wooden one. The wooden peg beat a monotonous tattoo as Gait crossed the room between the two guards, and came to a halt in front of the table at which sat Salsoun and Jimmy Christopher.

Gait had thrown one look in the direction of Daisy Gait, and then quickly looked away. Now he faced Salsoun, and his wrinkled face was red with rage. But he restrained himself, said nothing.

Salsoun lolled back in his chair, enjoying his own cleverness. "You are John Gait," he said. "That is your granddaughter. I have no time to waste, therefore I will tell you at once what I want you to do. You will go with this young captain, here, out to our fleet in the bay. You will pilot a destroyer of ours into the harbor for us. Is that clear?"

Gait's eyes flashed fire. "That's clear," he said. "But I won't do it!"

Salsoun grinned. "Oh, yes, you will!" He motioned to the two hussars holding the girl, and they dragged her forward.

Salsoun was watching the old pilot, carefully. But he spoke to the hussars. "This pilot is stubborn. Let us proceed with the girl."

One of the hussars grinned wickedly, and nodded. He withdrew his long bayonet from its scabbard, while the other hussar seized the girl by both arms from behind, holding her helpless.

"First the eyes," Salsoun commanded in a silky voice. "Put them out!"

Daisy Gait uttered a shriek, and began to struggle madly with her captor. Another hussar sprang forward to help the one who was holding her.

The girl continued to utter scream after scream. Her young, frightened voice cracked, and sobs wracked her body as she

THE SIEGE THAT BROUGHT THE BLACK DEATH

found herself helpless in the hands of the two Purple soldiers, with the bayonet's gleaming point close before her eyes.

John Gait had gone white. He made to spring forward, but one of the hussars knocked him down with a backhanded blow, and he went sprawling on the floor, shouting, "Damn you—*damn you!*"

Salsoun smiled thinly. "If you want to save her, you must speak quickly. Will you pilot our ship?"

Gait tried to get up from the floor, but a soldier put a heavy booted foot on his chest, held him there.

Daisy Gait had stopped struggling. She was panting for breath, but she cried out, "No, no, Granddaddy. Don't do it! Don't be a traitor. Let them kill me! I won't be the first to die for America!"

Jimmy Christopher had sat tautly through all this, watching with narrowed eyes, waiting for the moment when he would have to intervene. He had hoped that something would turn up to stop this inhuman thing that Salsoun was about to do, for he did not want to come out into the open yet. He had to find out the nature of the *coup* that was being planned for tomorrow.

Now he felt a quick stirring of admiration for this girl. Throughout the two years of the Purple Invasion he had seen, time after time, similar examples of personal bravery, heroism, martyrdom, for the cause of America's liberty. But that this eighteen-year-old girl should be ready to endure mutilation and death for the sake of her country, was something thrilling.

THE REST of the room had suddenly become quiet. The officers at the other tables were watching. The other American girls had paused, and were waiting with strained faces to see what would happen to Daisy Gait.

The old pilot's wooden leg was clubbing the floor ineffectually as he tried to rise against the pressure of the hussar's foot upon his chest.

Daisy Gait cried out again, "Don't do it, Granddaddy. They'll destroy New York with that ship, if you pilot it in. They're going to spread—"

That was as far as she got. Salsoun, purple with rage, sprang up and swung his hand in a back-handed blow that smashed into her mouth. Then he drew his sword, held it before the girl's face, pushing away the hussar with the bayonet. "I will blind her myself," he shouted to Gait, "if you refuse!"

His sword flicked forward, the point almost touching Daisy Gait's face. "One minute—"

It was then that Operator 5 intervened.

He pushed back his chair and arose, drawing his own sword with one smooth, continuous motion. Salsoun was on the other side of the table from him, and he could not reach the colonel to run him through. But he brought his sword around in a flashing arc, and struck down Salsoun's weapon.

Daisy Gait uttered a little gasp of relief, as the point fell away from her face.

Salsoun swung upon Jimmy Christopher, snarling. "You fool! I'll kill you for this!"

Jimmy smiled tightly. With his left hand, he thrust away the table from between them, and lunged at the colonel. The table fell with a crash, and the hussars side-stepped quickly to avoid it.

THE SIEGE THAT BROUGHT THE BLACK DEATH

Salsoun parried the lunge, and the two blades clashed. Salsoun shouted, "To me, hussars! Arrest this man!"

Jimmy Christopher attacked him fiercely, his blade flashing, swiftly moving, blindingly brilliant. Salsoun gave ground, on the defensive.

The officers and troopers in the room surged forward, shouting, tugging at swords, raising bayoneted rifles. They moved slowly however, unable to believe that anyone had actually dared to defy the chief of Purple intelligence—much less to attack him openly.

There was no doubt that Salsoun was a good swordsman. He had made his reputation in the Purple Army, as a remorseless duelist. It was a reckless man, indeed, who dared challenge the redoubtable Colonel Pretorius Salsoun.

But the colonel now met his match in Jimmy Christopher. Operator 5 had devoted years of his early life to the study of the art of swordsmanship. As a student of the renowned *salle d'armes* of the noted fencing master, Scherevesky, he had distinguished himself throughout Europe. His mastery of the *épée* had become a thing of pride to his teachers.

The officers who were now thronging to the assistance of Colonel Salsoun were treated to a sight they had never expected to witness—the sight of their most vaunted duelist giving ground before another's sword-point. Though they could not quite understand the cause of the quarrel between the intelligence chief of the Purple Empire and the dapper young naval captain, they were naturally going to the assistance of the colonel, because they knew him to be a favorite of the emperor. The hussars, too, thronged toward the two swordsmen at the colonel's cry for assistance, and in a moment Jimmy Christopher would have been overwhelmed by the weight of numbers.

But he was working fast, and with a purpose. As he forced Salsoun backward, he took a flashing instant of time to lunge sideways with his rapier at the big hussar whose foot was still pressing against Gait's chest. The Purple soldier tried to parry the thrust with this bayoneted rifle, but he was clumsily slow, and the point caught the man in the throat, sent him backward with red blood spurting out over his tunic.

John Gait, released from that pressure uttered a blood-curdling yell, and scrambled to his feet. Jimmy yelled to him in English, "Your granddaughter—get her out of here—to the launch at the dock!"

Gait was an old and canny sailor, quick-witted enough to grasp an idea in an emergency. He snatched up the rifle dropped by the hussar whom Jimmy had killed, and sprang at the two soldiers holding Daisy Gait.

Now, Jimmy Christopher had no time for anything else but Salsoun. The colonel was sweating with the effort of keeping Operator 5's sword point away from his heart, but, when he heard Jimmy speak in English, his eyes narrowed, and he exclaimed, "Operator 5! You are Operator 5! No one else can use a sword like that!"

He raised his voice in a great shout, to the others in the room. "This is Operator 5! Capture him!"

The other Purple officers, with the few hussars in the room, were almost upon the two duelists, and they raised a great shout

THE SIEGE THAT BROUGHT THE BLACK DEATH

of triumph, realizing that this would be the greatest catch of the war. There was no one in the world whom the Purple emperor more desired to capture than Operator 5.

They closed in upon him, and the nearest of them slashed at Jimmy with his sword. Jimmy saw that attempt out of the corner of his eye, and his rapier swished around in a terrific cut that slashed through the sleeve of the man's coat, almost severing his forearm.

The man fell back with a cry of agony. The others, urged on by Salsoun's rage-filled voice, closed in once more. They were certain of victory, for they knew that no one man could long withstand their numbers.

But now another element entered the fight. A long shrill *whoop* filled the room. Then a sudden avalanche of battling brawn and swinging clubs descended with the force of a whirlwind upon the backs of those Purple officers and hussars.

Jimmy Christopher's ten disguised seamen had now swung fiercely into action!

Their clubs rose and fell in savage rhythmic fury, smashing skulls, cracking arms, splintering swords. The young waitresses, who had been badgered by the officers, joined the fray, throwing cups, dishes, glasses, at the enemy. Now, too, half a dozen Americans emerged from the kitchen and from behind the bar where they had been compelled to work. They had long scullery knives, pokers, fire-tongs, any weapon that came to hand.

The room became a maelstrom of bitter raging battle.

THE PERSONAL courage of the Purple troops had always been a thing of mockery among Americans. Those troops of

Emperor Rudolph I always fought under rigid discipline, and with the aid of superior mechanical equipment. It was that military discipline and their heavy guns and tanks which had enabled them to trample victoriously over the country in the first place. But it was notorious that they had no heart for hand-to-hand conflict. They were not fighting for liberty, or for an ideal, nor yet to defend their homes against aggression. They were recruited from every corner of the world, from the slums and the cesspools of a degenerated European and Asiatic civilization.

Now that lack of personal courage was evident among them, as it had been evident in every battle, in every encounter where they had not been backed up by heavy barrage, or by tanks and airplanes. Under the fierce onslaught of the motley crew of Americans, they gave ground swiftly, more anxious to escape than to fight. True, they were in their own Occupied Territory, with their own army in control, and with numerous patrols within shouting distance. In fact, there was no doubt that half a dozen patrols must be rushing toward the restaurant even at this moment, and that the mad Americans must surely be overcome in the end. But they had no stomach for broken skulls or smashed arms and legs—to be gutted by the long scullery knives of the Americans who had rushed from the kitchen. There was no one among them who was willing to die in order that the American raiding-party might be held here until further reinforcements arrived. So they retreated, backing away from the attack, seeking to escape by the front door, or by the rear. Foremost among those to run was the great duelist, Colonel Pretorius Salsoun. He realized almost at once that his swordsmanship

THE SIEGE THAT BROUGHT THE BLACK DEATH

could never hope to match that of Operator 5. He recalled, in a swift flash of terror, that Operator 5 had once before engaged in a duel with one of the outstanding swordsman of the Purple Empire. He recalled too, that this man had died under Jimmy Christopher's rapier.

He had no wish to die that way. He was an ambitious man, and hoped some day, by currying favor with the emperor, to become the second man in the Purple Empire. Why should he throw away a valuable career in a gesture of bravery?

So he slipped back in the first crush of the attack by the Americans, and ran ignominiously for the door.

"Call the guard! Call the guard!" he shouted. "To arms! We are attacked!"

In truth, he, as well as the others there in the room, surely thought by this time that they were faced by a determined sortie in large numbers, staged by the American Army in New York. It never occurred to them that a party of eleven daring Americans could have had the temerity to stage a raid like this, against a city held by a whole Purple Division.

Now the exodus began in earnest. The officers and troopers streamed out of there, as if the devil himself were at their heels. The Americans spurred them on, slashing them, clubbing them, hacking at them. They left several of their number wounded and disabled on the floor. Within ten minutes of the time when Jimmy Christopher had sprung up to the defense of Daisy Gait, the room was cleared, and the Americans were in possession of the restaurant. John Gait and his granddaughter had not run, as Jimmy had advised. Daisy had joined the other

OPERATOR 5

girls in the attack on the enemy, and the old, one-legged pilot had reddened his bayonet with the blood of many of the Purple officers. Now he came hobbling over to Jimmy, grinning in smug satisfaction. The other Americans raised a shout of victory, and thronged about Jimmy.

They were flushed with their easy success, and they longed for more action. "What'll we do now, Operator 5?" they shouted. "Let's take the town!"

Operator 5's eyes sparkled with pride. These men were typical of the America for which he was fighting. It was this spirit that had checkmated the Purple emperor time and again, when he had been on the edge of victory through superior war equipment. Such raw courage, Jimmy reflected, could never be entirely subjugated. But now he had a real problem on his hands. Instead of his original ten men, he had almost twenty-five men, and some fifteen girls. He must get them safely to the launch, and out of Hoboken—but how? The patrols would be thronging into the streets, and surely there would be a company of guards rushing here from the garrison barracks. They must hurry, or their retreat would be cut off.

There was one more thing which he must do before leaving. He still had to find Diane, to get her safely out of the ferry boat where she was lying wounded. Now, his blood was racing at the promise of that!

HIS QUICK cool glance surveyed the possibilities of the situation. He saw that his men were armed now, not only with their original clubs and knives, but also with rifles, swords and bayonets dropped by the fleeing and wounded Purple troop-

THE SIEGE THAT BROUGHT THE BLACK DEATH

ers. It was possible that they could fight their way through the enemy to the launch.

But there was the chance that the launch might be taken by the hussars. The five men remaining there might be rushed. He was pretty sure, of course, that they were warned, for they could not have helped hearing the fight, and they would see the commotion in the streets, guess that the landing party was in trouble. The sensible thing for them to do, of course, would be to cast off and escape. But Jimmy knew his men. They would wait.

He formed them into a double line, with Daisy Gait and the other girls in the middle. Then, with John Gait at his side, he led them loping out of the restaurant.

The street outside was filling up with troops, and, as soon as they appeared, a scattering volley thundered at them. They had expected this, and Jimmy dropped to the ground, with the others following his example. The volley passed over their heads harmlessly, and, in the next instant, Jimmy Christopher was on his feet, shouting, "Charge!"

He led the mad rush, directly at the thin line of Purple troops facing them. Those hussars prepared grimly to send another hail of lead into the gallant Americans. Already, other troops were rushing up from the garrison headquarters. These men knew by now that there were only a few of the raiders.

Jimmy could see Salsoun, at the end of the line of hussars blocking their way to the river. Salsoun had his sword in the air, ready to give the signal to fire.

Jimmy's lips tightened grimly. This was the end. They would

be mowed down mercilessly before they could even reach the enemy to engage them hand-to-hand.

He was sorry that he had led his ten men into the trap, and for the girls, who would die here with them.

He drew his own revolver, firing as he ran. But he clearly saw Salsoun's sword start to come down in the signal to fire.

Just then, from behind the Purple line, a machine gun began to chatter!

CHAPTER 7
FIGHT TO A FINISH

FOR ONE dreadful moment, Jimmy Christopher thought that the Purple guards had brought up machine guns to mow them down. That would have been the end of their small company. John Gait, who hobbled beside him, thought the same, for the old man began to curse very fluently, saltily.

But Gait stopped cursing, and gaped with mouth wide open, as the line of Purple soldiers began to crumple.

"*Hey!*" he shouted. "Glory be! Those guns—"

Jimmy Christopher didn't let him finish. "Come on!" he shouted to those behind him. "It's our own boys from the launch!"

The five men from the launch had not waited passively while the landing party bore the brunt of the fighting. They had broken out the sub-machine guns from the launch's arms closet, and three of them, thus armed, had sallied into the streets leaving only two men to defend the launch.

THE SIEGE THAT BROUGHT THE BLACK DEATH

It was their clattering guns which had crumpled the Purple line.

Jimmy Christopher saw Salsoun running away down a side street with the few surviving Purple officers, but he did not bother to pursue them. He led his party forward to meet the three gunners from the launch. The three men, one of whom was a junior officer named Drummond, stared in wonder at the strange assemblage of sailors, cooks, bartenders and waitresses who followed Operator 5.

Jimmy didn't give them time to answer questions.

"Back to the river!" he ordered. "We've got to get going before the garrison troops arrive!"

Already, they could hear the pounding hooves of a cavalry contingent drumming on the cobblestones somewhere behind them. The backfire of a troop truck sounded dangerously nearby.

The machine gunners swung in behind Jimmy Christopher and John Gait, while Lieutenant Drummond brought up the rear to make sure no stragglers were left behind to be captured by the enemy.

They were still almost a block and a half away from the launch, when Jimmy saw a mounted patrol of Purple guards riding swiftly down the waterfront toward the dock where the launch was tied up. The riders turned out onto the dock, evidently intending to ride right up to the launch. But a burst of machine-gun fire from the gun mounted on the cabin cut down half of them, and the rest retreated precipitately.

Jimmy ran more swiftly now, helping John Gait with one hand. The old man was handicapped by his wooden leg, and begged Jimmy to leave him behind so that he would not endanger the rest of the group. Operator 5 would not hear of it.

They were passing a huge old warehouse on the street leading to the river, when Jimmy Christopher heard a bedlam of cries from within, followed by the sounds of shouting, cursing, and blows being struck.

Jimmy's eyes narrowed, and he stopped short. The entrance to the warehouse was directly opposite, and he could see that a sentry who, had been outside, was just rushing in, swinging his gun forward as if to fire at someone within.

The sentry fired just once, and then was overwhelmed by a wild crowd of ragged-looking men who literally engulfed him, stampeding over him into the street—but not before one of their number had wrenched the rifle from the sentry's hand. Old John Gait exclaimed excitedly, "It's the American civilians in the labor battalion! They're quartered here—over two thousand of them. They've broken loose!"

THE MEN who streamed out of those barracks were gaunt, ill-dressed, unkempt. Many had not been shaven for weeks on end. They were unarmed, except for a few, who had the weapons of the guards they had overpowered. These men had been kept virtual prisoners, locked up in the barracks every night, and compelled to perform back-breaking toil from sunrise to sunset. Yet their spirit was alive and strong, and there was no fear among them.

When they saw Jimmy Christopher's uniform, and the uniforms of his disguised sailors, they made to rush at them.

THE SIEGE THAT BROUGHT THE BLACK DEATH

But old John Gait shouted in his stentorian sea-going voice, "Belay there! This is Operator 5!"

The labor battalion brought up short, and a huge Negro with the rippling muscles of an Atlas, grinned, pawing Jimmy Christopher all over. "I'm Nate Schley," he said. "I was heavyweight contender for the title before the Purple Invasion. We heard there was fightin' in the town, an' figured our boys was attacking—so we broke out."

Jimmy Christopher stared about him at the gathering throng of prisoners who where forming a great circle about him and his small group.

They were shouting, "Lead, Operator 5! Lead us!"

Jimmy glanced from John Gait to the Negro, Nate Schley. "This was no attack," he explained to the ex-prizefighter. "There are only fifteen of us, from a small launch. I can't even take you all off with me. The launch would founder with a hundred men!"

Nate Schley's face fell. "We're not goin' back to them barracks, Operator 5. We've had enough o' that. If you don't lead us outa here, we'll go out an' fight those Purple devils with our bare hands until they kill us to the last man. We been waitin' a long time to strike a blow for America!"

Jimmy was touched by Nate Schley's ardor and his eagerness to fight. The two thousand men, who thronged the street, backed up his words with vociferous shouts.

Lieutenant Drummond pushed his way up to Jimmy. "There's a squadron of enemy cavalry coming down Ferry Street, sir," he reported. "They're making slow progress because people are throwing bricks at them from the housetops. It looks like the whole civilian population has risen against the enemy. But there's a large body of infantry from the barracks deploying toward us down every side street. In ten minutes, our street to the river will be cut off—"

Operator 5's eyes were glistening. "We're not going to retreat, Drummond!" he announced. "We're going to take this town!"

Drummond stared at Operator 5. "You're mad, sir! What good are all these men against the trained regiments of the Purple Army—and without guns or ammunition?"

"They've got something the other side lacks, Drummond," Jimmy told him. "They have *spirit!*"

He swung about, and suddenly was the crisp, efficient strategist who had saved the day more than once for the American cause. He issued orders that followed each other with the rapid fire of a machine gun.

"John Gait, you will take a hundred men and hurry back to the launch," he said. "Break out all the arms you find there, and equip your men. Keep only ten rounds of ammunition per man, and send all the rest back here to me. Now get going!"

He sent Drummond with five hundred men, back into the side street along which the cavalry was approaching. With him, he sent one machine gunner. "Rip up the pavement, and make a barricade. Hold that cavalry there for twenty minutes, at any cost. I'm sending Nate Schley around to take them in the flank. We'll wipe out that cavalry detachment!"

He gave the negro prizefighter another five hundred men, and instructed him to take the riverfront down to a street that would bring him into the flank of the cavalry. "There are some

THE SIEGE THAT BROUGHT THE BLACK DEATH

JIMMY CHRISTOPHER

narrow alleys over there. Take the narrowest, where the cavalry won't be able to operate efficiently against you. Take the men with bayonets. Let them give their rifles to other men. With cold steel, in the narrow alley, they should not be at any disadvantage against the mounted Uhlans."

Nate Schley showed his white teeth in a broad grin. "Leave it to us, sir!"

OPERATOR 5 found himself left with more than a thousand men, practically all unarmed, except for thirty or forty who had rifles, knives, and odd implements hastily picked up. "Boys," he called out to them, "ours is going to be the toughest assignment. We're going up against the infantry—and the machine guns!"

Instead of being frightened at the prospect, they cheered. Jimmy still had one machine gun from the launch. In a few moments, half a dozen of John Gait's men came running back from the riverfront, carrying some fifteen or twenty spare rifles which they had found in the launch's arms chest. They distributed these among Jimmy's men, together with the spare ammunition.

Before starting out to meet the advancing enemy, Jimmy Christopher detailed thirty men to go to the old ferry boat and find Diane. He would have much preferred to go after her himself, but this thing, which had begun as a daring raid, had developed into something of such great proportions that he could not leave it. He reflected grimly that it was like having a tiger by the tail.

It was a mad, suicidal undertaking. There were at least two full divisions of Purple troops in and around Hoboken at this time.

THE SIEGE THAT BROUGHT THE BLACK DEATH

That meant thirty thousand men, equipped with rifles, machine guns, artillery—against two thousand ragged individuals, most of them having nothing but their bare hands with which to put up a fight.

But Jimmy Christopher knew the temper of the American civilian population of the Occupied Territories. They would risk everything, attempt anything, if only there was some small chance of breaking the dreadful yoke of servitude which the Purple conquerors had placed upon their necks.

This spontaneous uprising would spread throughout the town and neighboring territory. Within an hour, he knew, every man and woman within reach of the fighting would be here, ready to join in the battle against the might of the Purple Empire. He had seen it happen time and time again—in Pittsburgh, Philadelphia, and even in New York.

But now the chances against success were too large. Though he spoke encouragingly to these men, he was well aware that if the approaching infantry had only two pieces of light ordnance, they would be able to sweep the streets clean of his disorganized, unarmed mob. And if they could, by some miracle, succeed in holding this sector against the enemy, there were countless additional Purple divisions in Jersey City, as well as in the country north of Hoboken, where they were pushing back the American troops on the Patterson Plank Road.

There was only one hope of salvation, and he took it. He chose twenty men at random, to whom he spoke swiftly, succinctly, outlining the precarious situation in which they found themselves.

"Our only chance is to bring up American troops from somewhere, to back us up," he told them. "I want ten of you men to volunteer to commandeer any kind of boats at the waterfront, and cross the river to New York. Notify General Ferrara of what is happening, and ask him to try to send a strong force back with you. Let him turn out as many men as he can ferry across. The other ten of you—I want you to try to get through the enemy lines to Major Slocum, commanding our troops on the Patterson Plank Road. Ask him to start a drive southward, to divert the enemy from us here in Hoboken. If we can get them to do that, it'll force the enemy to send troops to meet Slocum's drive, and it'll relieve the pressure here. Who knows—with a ghost of a break, we may succeed in driving the enemy out of Hoboken!"

The twenty men agreed to undertake the dangerous mission at once.

When they left, Jimmy spread his thousand men out into all the sidestreets by which the enemy infantry was approaching. **ALREADY, THE** close-packed troops of the enemy were pouring down toward the riverfront, and Jimmy at once ordered his machine gunner to get into action. A barricade had already been thrown up, and the gunner took his position behind that, flanked by half a dozen riflemen.

Almost before he was set, the enemy were upon the barricade, and he started his gun chattering. The first burst threw the enemy ranks back upon themselves in confusion, and the unarmed Americans leaped out from behind the barricade, with nothing but their bare fists. They fell upon the momentar-

THE SIEGE THAT BROUGHT THE BLACK DEATH

ily disorganized enemy with such wild fury that the mercenary infantry began to push back.

The Americans fought with a concentrated savagery that more than made up for their lack of arms. The few with bayonets and rifles opened the way for the others, who punched, kicked, gouged, choked, dying under the swords and bayonets of the enemy, but killing a goodly number themselves.

Americans fell fast, cluttering the narrow street. But always there were more to take their places. Those who fell were sure to carry some of the enemy with them. Jimmy Christopher wanted to recall them behind the barricade, to have them take refuge while the machine gunner went to work again. But they were deaf and blind with fury and hatred. They remembered the long miserable days spent in the labor battalions, the scenes of torture and killing they had witnessed in the streets, mothers, daughters, wives, denied, tortured, murdered, by these Purple ruffians. They smashed into those Purple columns with only one object in mind—to avenge those memories that burned white hot within them.

Jimmy Christopher had kept two hundred men down near the river, as a reserve. Now he sent fifty of these to percolate into the buildings along the streets in which the fighting was heaviest. They were to climb to the roofs at a point where they could command the enemy, and drop bricks, pieces of cornice, or anything they could find down, upon the Purple troops. Those men went to their tasks with a will.

Operator 5 noticed that somehow his reserve force was growing larger, instead of being depleted. Men were drifting into that reserve from out of the darkness, by twos or threes, and sometimes by the dozen. Word had spread throughout Hoboken that the Americans were staging an attack. Recruits were thronging from every section. Men who had lain in hiding for long months in dark and noisome cellars; men who had secreted themselves in abandoned buildings and under the pilings of docks; men who had lived on the outskirts of the town, venturing in only at night to visit their families—all of these were flocking to the banner of revolt.

One group of about two dozen men appeared as if from nowhere, lugging with them a great box that took six to carry They opened it and proudly displayed a store of hand grenades.

"We got them off a military truck that we waylaid in the street," they explained. These men also had brand new Schlossman-Krieg automatic rifles which they had taken from the crew of the truck, together with plenty of ammunition.

Those Schlossman-Kriegs were sharpshooters' rifles, fitted with telescopic sights, equipped with silencers and with a drum that permitted them to fire twenty-five rounds without reloading. They had been recently developed and placed into large-scale operation by the small-arms factories of the great Krieg Works in Europe, and they were part of the first consignment of new war material which had been delivered to Emperor Rudolph by the Fleet during the past week.

Jimmy was thankful for them. He sent the men with those rifles into the streets to enter buildings and snipe from the upper windows. He immediately organized a hand-grenade corps to join the front ranks of the Americans fighting in the streets.

THE SIEGE THAT BROUGHT THE BLACK DEATH

It was perhaps those hand grenades which definitely decided the Battle of Hoboken.* There were only some forty of the grenades in the box, but they enabled the Americans to take

---

* AUTHOR'S NOTE: Military experts have made exhaustive studies of every detail of the Battle of Hoboken, endeavoring to find the common denominator of victory in battle through a study of this particular engagement. The reason for all this research is that the Battle of Hoboken is a military phenomenon defying any sort of logic. By all the laws of warfare, the suicidal attempt of the ragged group of men under Operator 5's leadership should have been an utter failure—in fact, was doomed to defeat before a single shot was fired. It is incomprehensible—as well as against all the possibilities—that two thousand starved, unarmed men should attain a victory over two divisions of trained troops fighting with the most modern equipment available to a battle unit Of course, there were certain elements in favor of Operator 5. One was the spirit of his men, and their desperation. The other was the fact that all of the fighting took place in narrow streets where the discipline and formation of trained troops could not show to the best advantage. It didn't matter, for instance, in the fighting that took place in Ferry Street, that there were some five thousand enemy troops massed against less than a thousand Americans; for the only effective fighting that could be done was by those in the front ranks. But the Americans might even then have been routed, had it not been for the fortunate appearance of those hand grenades. Accurately thrown, they fell among the thickest of the enemy troops, killing and maiming hundreds of them with each explosion. The Purple hussars had no stomach for this, and they tried to escape from further grenades, rather than to attack the men who were throwing them. The ensuing confusion was the opening the Americans needed.

the offensive on a larger scale. The grenade throwers would hurl one of their "eggs" into a lane crowded with enemy infantry. The ensuing explosion would so break up the enemy ranks that the Americans could cut right through them, picking up discarded weapons as they went.

How long that battle took, Jimmy Christopher never knew. He was aware only of constant pressure, of a wild state of urgency existing during every crowded moment of it. He issued orders by the hundred, sending men to bolster up this street, or shifting men from one spot to another, or organizing a hospital corps to carry wounded men back to the launch where they could be easily removed from shore if the battle should turn against them.

He remembered the triumphant return of Lieutenant Drummond, leading his men astride horses taken from the cavalry contingent, which they had virtually wiped out. Drummond's men were well armed now, with the loot from the cavalry, and Jimmy Christopher immediately threw them into the battle, sending them down along the waterfront to charge a company of enemy infantry that trickled out of the fighting in the side streets to re-form its ranks.

Drummond's horsemen broke them up in short order.

Fires were starting in several near-by parts of the town, caused by the grenades. These raged unchecked, while the hourly growing forces of Operator 5 drove the Purple troops back block by block. But now, the main force of the garrison from the barracks was swinging into the fight, and the enemy had stopped retreating.

Two six-inch howitzers appeared in one of the streets, and

THE SIEGE THAT BROUGHT THE BLACK DEATH

the enemy swiftly set them up under the protection of successive waves of infantry charges that kept the Americans from reaching the gunners.

But they never got to firing those howitzers. Some of the Americans were up on the roofs of the buildings overlooking the gun crews, and they dropped three well placed grenades that wiped out the entire crews, and caused tremendous explosions of the shells that had been brought up to feed the guns.

Now there suddenly came the clear shrill notes of a bugle, and the Americans raised cheer after cheer. A man came breathlessly running up to Jimmy Christopher to announce that a brigade of Fletcher's Jersey Cavalry had just arrived from the Patterson Plank Road and were attacking the rear of the enemy.

More and more American troops poured into Hoboken, and, an hour later, the enemy had been driven out of the town. The Battle of Hoboken was won!

THE FIRST signs of dawn were already apparent in the sky as Operator 5 called in his jubilant men. The battle had lasted throughout the night, but Jimmy Christopher gave them no rest now. He was eager to consolidate the position, for he was certain that Emperor Rudolph would lose no time in moving his main force up from Jersey City in a determined effort to retake the town.

Jimmy took stock of their supplies, and found that there were rifles enough to supply all his men—now numbering close to seven thousand, together with two million rounds of ammunition. They had also captured fourteen six-inch howitzers, eight 155 mm guns, and two batteries of huge sixteen-inch guns which the enemy had been mounting on the shore to command New York City.

He immediately set men to work to change the position of these big cannon so that they could command the Upper Bay, in case the Purple Fleet got through. There were no guns in New York City equaling these in size, and it was the first time since the siege of New York had begun that the Americans began to have any hope of stopping the great warships of the Purple Fleet.

A semaphore was rigged up, and Jimmy flashed the news across to Hank Sheridan and General Ferrara. Then, after having congratulated Nate Schley and Lieutenant Drummond, he left them in charge of further organization, and went to find Diane.

HE BOARDED the launch elated in spirit, though he was dog-weary in body. He had not slept all night, and he looked forward to a day full of urgent action. He had gone without sleep for days on end in the past, however, and could do it again. What he wanted most now, was to see Diane Elliot, make sure she was all right, and then have her transferred over to a base hospital in New York, where her wound could be properly attended to.

But when he mounted to the deck of the launch he saw that something was wrong. Though the men on board, including old John Gait, were rejoicing in the victory, there was a peculiar air of restraint about them—a suspicious furtiveness with which they looked at him—that caused him at once to feel uneasy.

It was John Gait who broke the news to him.

"Look here, Operator 5," the pilot said haltingly. "I—I can't just figure on how to tell you this." He halted unhappily.

"Diane!" Jimmy interrupted. "What's happened to her?" He

THE SIEGE THAT BROUGHT THE BLACK DEATH

felt suddenly cold, deflated. He put a rough hand on the pilot's shoulder. "Quick, man—what is it?"

Gait lowered his eyes. "We—we don't know, Operator 5. We—we can't find her. She's not on the ferry boat!"

"But she was wounded!" Jimmy protested. "She couldn't have gone off by herself. She wouldn't have done it even if she could. She must have known I'd come after her!"

Gait shook his head. "She's not there, Jimmy. We found the place where Tim Donovan left her, all right. There's traces of blood on the bench and on the deck of the boat. We could even trace the blood—a separate trail where she came in, and another where she left. The one going out leads right off the deck, and onto the dock—and that's where it ends!"

Jimmy Christopher's shoulders sagged. The men all gathered about him, sympathetically. His face was white, drained of blood.

On the shore, a bugle sounded, and the American flag was run up over the custom house to replace the hideous emblem of the Purple Empire which had floated there through the night. But Jimmy Christopher did not raise his eyes. He was thinking of Diane Elliot somewhere in Jersey, alone and wounded—perhaps even now a prisoner of the enemy. The whole victory seemed hollow to him.

His semaphore to Hank Sheridan across the river was answered. A runner brought it from shore. It read, "Congratulations, Operator 5. Am sending more troops to help you consolidate your position. Go to it."

But Jimmy scarcely saw the words of the message. This was a bitter ending, indeed, to the glorious battle he had fought through the night. He was wondering how he would face Tim Donovan and tell him that he had neglected to look for Diane all through the night, until morning, and then found she was gone.

"Why didn't you let me know before?" he demanded of Gait.

The sailor shrugged. "We were all too busy for that, Operator 5. I didn't want to disturb you with news like that. There wasn't anything you could have done about it, anyway."

Jimmy nodded, put a hand on Gait's shoulder. "That's right, I don't blame you. But now—" he sighed—"I'll have to start looking for her all over—"

His words were drowned by a sudden upheaval of sound that veritably blanketed the city and river. Thunderous detonations of mighty guns rocked the very air about them. Whining shells screamed high overhead. Explosions sent the currents of the river into crazy zigzag patterns that twisted the launch about as if it had been a toy canoe.

Gait pointed with a shaking finger out toward the bay.

"The Purple Fleet!" he shouted. "They're bombarding New York!"

It was true. Every gun on those great ships out there in the bay was belching its deadly message of destruction. Smashing concussions deafened them as the great shells struck their objectives in the city streets across the river.

Jimmy Christopher's lips tightened. For the moment, he forgot about Diane. There was no defense against this bombardment. In an hour the city would be a shambles, and all the work of reconstruction would be once more destroyed.

THE SIEGE THAT BROUGHT THE BLACK DEATH

This was Emperor Rudolph's answer to the Battle of Hoboken!

CHAPTER 8
THE EMPEROR'S ALLY

IN A chair made entirely of chased gold, in the throne room of imperial headquarters in Jersey City, sat Rudolph I, emperor of the Purple Empire, master of Europe and Asia, and self-styled emperor of America.

Rudolph's gaunt and sallow visage was twisted into a frown of disapproval as he gazed with black, kindling eyes upon the wretched figure of Colonel Pretorius Salsoun, chief of imperial intelligence.

Salsoun was writhing, figuratively and literally. For ten minutes now he had listened to a tongue-lashing of which only the emperor was capable. He stood there, eyes cast down, not daring to lift his head to meet the gaze of his master.

At the right side of the emperor's chair stood the prime minister of the Purple Empire, Baron Julian Flexner. Upon the emperor's left stood two uniformed, high-ranking officers—Marshal Kremer, commander-in-chief of all the armies of the empire, and Admiral Ugo von der Selz, admiral of the Imperial Navy.

The only other person who was seated was a dark, exotic woman who occupied a chair placed at right angles to the emperor's throne. She was smoking a long Turkish cigarette, in a long amber holder. Her crossed legs revealed a shimmering expanse of black silk stockings, and her gossamer, black dress showed more of the creamy skin of her shoulders and breasts than was good for an impressionable man like the emperor to see. This woman was known to the courtiers only by the name of Mistra.

Whence she had come from originally, no one could tell. A few months ago, she had appeared in the train of the Mongol general, Shan Hi Mung, one of the powerful war lords who had followed Rudolph to the conquest of America. Shan Hi Mung had, at one time, made Rudolph a prisoner, endeavoring to trade with him—offering the emperor his freedom if Rudolph would promise to let him have America for himself, and be content to rule over the rest of the world.

But Rudolph had outwitted Shan Hi Mung, and regained his freedom, with the aid of Baron Flexner. Shan Hi Mung's armies of fierce Mongols were still in the service of the emperor, marching south against New York City even now. But Shan Hi Mung did not know—that the girl, Mistra, had elected to go with Rudolph, choosing to be the mistress of the emperor of the world, rather than of a mere Mongol war lord.

Now, as she watched the proceedings, she allowed the smoke of the cigarette to trickle lazily through her nostrils. There was a thin, mysterious smile on her red lips as she listened to Rudolph's tirade against Salsoun.

Outside, the thunder of the continuous cannonade, which had lasted for almost two hours now, shook the walls of the building, and sent waves of sound percolating through the room. The fleet in the harbor had been steadily shelling New York

THE SIEGE THAT BROUGHT THE BLACK DEATH

and Hoboken since morning, without much retaliation from the Americans—for the few sixteen-inch guns which they had captured, were no match for the eighteen-inch guns mounted on the powerful battleships in the bay.

BUT NOW no one in the room had ears for that thunderous bombardment. They were listening to Rudolph's high-pitched voice as he leaned forward in his throne and shook a finger in Salsoun's face.

"You are an incompetent bungler, Salsoun! Your idea may have been a good one, but you bungled it. I ought to have you beheaded—no, that would be too good for you!" He glanced across at the woman. His glance softened, became almost lascivious as his eyes traveled over her generously revealed body. "What do you suggest for this bungler, Mistra?"

She shrugged daintily. "You could hang him by his two big toes, sire, and then run bayonets through his body. He would last a long time that way, and be very amusing."

Salsoun shivered, and wiped sweat from his eyes with the back of his hand. He dropped to one knee. "Be merciful, Your Majesty. Give me a chance to redeem myself. It was not my fault that the plan failed. It was this devil of an Operator 5. I thought he was the officer that von der Selz had sent me. Next time, I shall not make such a mistake."

Rudolph's lips puffed out in rage. "Bah! The only reason I hesitate, is because you have served me well in the past. But I never allow more than one blunder." He turned to his prime minister. "What do you say, Flexner?"

Baron Julian Flexner had been watching Salsoun with a thin,

satirical smile. He had been fearful of Salsoun. The colonel had risen too fast in the emperor's favor, and Flexner had often wondered whether the intelligence chief did not harbor the ambition of replacing him as prime minister. He bent low and whispered in Rudolph's ear.

Rudolph's face grew redder as he listened. He nodded, his lips tightening cruelly. He spoke to the miserable colonel. "Flexner is right, Salsoun. He says that your blundering has cost us the loss of Hoboken, together with all the war stores there. Not only that, you virtually had Operator 5 in your hands, and allowed him to escape—not only to escape, but to drive our troops from Hoboken."

Salsoun was shivering now, as with the ague. "Mercy, sire," he begged. "I swear to search for this Operator 5, and to bring him to you, if you will but spare me!"

Rudolph twirled his moustache. "You know how I hate that Operator 5. He has tricked me time and again, made a laughing-stock of me. Were it not for him, America would be mine today. And *you* let him slip through your fingers!" He clenched his fists. "No! No mercy for you! You shall hang by your toes, as Mistra suggests!"

He raised a hand, and motioned to two guards at the door. "Take him to the dungeons below. Tomorrow, we will amuse ourselves with him!"

Salsoun's voice broke, as he begged for mercy. But the two guards dragged him out under the amused glance of the woman, Mistra. She laughed.

"It will be very good entertainment," she said.

THE SIEGE THAT BROUGHT THE BLACK DEATH

Flexner relaxed with a satisfied smile. He had won. Many men had tried to displace him as prime minister; many men had plotted against him. But he had remained in his position longer than any other prime minister. He was safe now for awhile, until some other ambitious man came to challenge his position. Flexner might have wished that Salsoun could be disposed of with less pain and agony to the colonel. The prime minister was not himself a cruel man, and did not like to see suffering in others. But with a master such as Rudolph, he dared not intercede for anyone. There was always the danger that he, himself, might be delivered to the tender mercies of the executioner.

RUDOLPH WAS indulging in his usual habit of biting his fingernails and cursing in a low voice. "Why," he demanded of Flexner, "is it impossible to catch that Operator 5? I have offered the overlordship of a whole province to the man who captures him for me. Is that not enough?" He bit his nails now.

"It is enough, sire," Flexner told him soothingly. "Everyone of your subjects would gladly bring him to you without reward, to make you happy. But the man is too clever. However—" he paused, let his voice grow mysterious—"there is always the chance that this Operator 5 may slip up."

Rudolph's eyes gleamed. "You know something, Flexner? Quick, man! What is it? I can tell by your voice that you have something up your sleeve!"

The baron shrugged. "It is only a chance, sire. I have not verified it yet. But there was a young woman brought in this morning. She was found by a patrol in Hoboken, wandering in delirium just outside the old ferry dock there. She was wounded and in high fever, and did not know what she was doing. Apparently, she had been hiding in the ferry, and had wandered out in her delirium. She collapsed just as the patrol found her, and they have brought her here. From her description, I hope she is the one I think she is. If so, sire, then we shall have a great magnet by which to draw Operator 5 into our net."

Rudolph had listened with bounding eagerness. "Where is this girl? Who—do you think she is?"

"They have her outside in the corridor, sire—on a stretcher, and still unconscious. Her wound has been dressed, but she has been given a hypodermic. The wound itself is not bad, and she should recover consciousness by evening. May I have her brought in?"* He bowed very low.

---

* Author's Note: Many persons have been too harsh in their judgment of Baron Julian Flexner. It is quite true that he did many things that were despicable; but it must be remembered that he served a master who would not have hesitated to consign him to the harshest torture at the first sign of Flexner's disapproval or disobedience to the cruel whims of this crudest of monarchs. Besides, it must be borne in mind that the baron's beautiful young daughter was with him at court, and that she constituted a sort of hostage. Even had Flexner possessed the courage to defy Rudolph for himself, he must have realized that the emperor would cause his daughter to suffer, too. There are many instances where Baron Flexner exerted his influence in devious ways to ease the punishments which Rudolph imposed. He points to many of these cases in his memoirs, but he does so in a very guarded manner. To really understand this wily minister who managed to maintain his position of prime minister, despite the vagaries of his emperor, and despite the

THE SIEGE THAT BROUGHT THE BLACK DEATH

"Yes, yes! Quickly!"

The baron crossed the room and whispered to a guard, and a moment later a stretcher-wagon was wheeled into the room. Upon it, under a white sheet which was rivaled by the whiteness of her face, lay Diane Elliot.

The attendants wheeled the stretcher close up to the throne and Rudolph half-rose in his seat in his excitement. His small eyes glued to Diane's face, mirrored the lustful hate of a man of unbridled passions.

"Yes, yes!" he exclaimed gloatingly. "It is she. It is Operator 5's woman—the Elliot girl!" He turned to his prime minister.

---

nets of intrigue with which the court was honeycombed, one must study Flexner's memoirs, and read between the lines. Those memoirs were written day by day, and he must have lived in constant dread that they would be found by some spy and turned over to the emperor. Therefore whatever he wrote was written guardedly, and often with double meanings. Heretofore, historians have failed to catch those double meanings, and they have failed to understand him because they did not fully understand the events they recounted. But I have been particularly fortunate, in that I have been able to study those memoirs in the light of the knowledge I have gained from the diary of Operator 5 as well as from the notes of Diane Elliot and Tim Donovan. With that additional knowledge I can safely say that Flexner hated his monarch wholeheartedly, and that his instincts revolted at the hideous cruelties that were inflicted upon innocent men and women. But he served the emperor, partly because he was a coward for himself and for his daughter, and partly because he nursed the ambition of one day seeing the Purple Empire grow great and powerful under another, more merciful ruler.

OPERATOR 5

"This is wonderful Flexner—wonderful! It is better fortune than I had hoped for. Flexner, you have done very well. You may have anything you wish!"

Flexner bowed low. He murmured, "I wish only the pleasure and privilege of serving you faithfully, sire!"

Rudolph was so beside himself with joy that he actually patted the baron on the shoulder. "Good, Flexner, good. You are worth more to me than all my generals and admirals and intelligence chiefs."

Flexner threw a wry side-glance at crusty old Marshal Kremer and at Admiral von der Selz who stood on the emperor's other side. "I am happy that you approve, sire. Shall we send this girl to a hospital until she recovers—"

"Hospital? No! She goes into the dungeons. Tomorrow, when she is conscious, we will have her up again!" The emperor was rubbing his hands. "We shall make her pay with hours and days of agony for the things that Operator 5 has done to me!"

The woman, Mistra, stirred interestedly. Her cat's eyes swept over the supine, unconscious form of Diane. "That will be very interesting, too," she drawled. "I suggest hanging her on hooks, by her breasts. I imagine that would be very painful. I have always wanted to try it on someone."

Rudolph waved the attendants away. "Take her down to the dungeons. Have a physician attend her. Let him see that she is conscious, and able to understand what goes on by tomorrow morning!"

The attendants wheeled the stretcher out of the room.

THE SIEGE THAT BROUGHT THE BLACK DEATH

The deep booming of the guns was still audible, beating a reverberating refrain.

Rudolph smiled with inward satisfaction. "Things are going better and better!" He turned to Admiral von der Selz. "And now, von der Selz, what about this plan of Salsoun's that failed last night? Are you ready to carry it out without him?"

The admiral bowed. "Yes, sire. The destroyer is ready, with the cages and their—occupants. Under cover of the barrage from the fleet, the ship is moving up the harbor, escorted by tugs which take soundings as they go. Ordinarily, we could not do this, because the Americans would have been able to blow the tugs out of the water. But now we need only to continue the barrage for another two hours, and the destroyer will have picked her way into the harbor. She will dock at the Battery and presto—" the admiral snapped his fingers—"the trick is done. The Americans will be so busy and so frightened after that, that they will have no time to think of Shan Hi Mung's Mongol Army, which is marching down upon them from the north!"

Rudolph chuckled. "It is a good idea. It will kill two birds with one stone. It will cripple the Americans, and it will help me to be rid of that Mongol."

CHAPTER 9
COMING OF THE
BLACK DEATH

THE STREETS of New York City were as bare of life, as if a tornado had swept them clean. And, indeed, it was more than a tornado whose scourge was now whirling about the city to the accompaniment of the whining screech of shells being fired from huge guns at the rate of fifty per minute.

It was a nightmare.

Nature, in the moments of her greatest fury, has never produced a hell equal to that produced by the machinery evolved out of the mind of man. No destructive cyclone, no hurricane, no earthquake, has ever equaled the destructive force of a modern barrage laid down by the broadsides of huge ships of war.

The concussions of the high-explosive shells kept repeating with such inhuman frequency that men were deafened, driven mad, stunned. Huge craters appeared in the sidewalks, and masonry tumbled from the sides of steel buildings to add their tithe of rumbling roar to the maelstrom of detonations that rocked the city. The American shore batteries, both on the New York and the Hoboken side, were silent, utterly destroyed in the first hour of the bombardment.

All of the civilian population had taken shelter in cellars constructed for just this purpose. Not a dog was in the streets.

The armed defense force was holed in dugouts and pill-boxes, waiting wearily for the barrage to lift—waiting and wondering whether they would be able to stem the attack which must inevitably follow.

In a room high up in the Empire State Building—one of the few structures still standing—a group of tight-lipped men were holding a council of war.

There was President Sheridan, and General Ferrara, and a dozen staff officers. Operator 5 was with them.

THE SIEGE THAT BROUGHT THE BLACK DEATH

Jimmy Christopher had crossed over in the launch under the first wave of the barrage, leaving the Jersey shore in the capable hands of Colonel Slocum and Lieutenant Drummond. He had wanted to be here, where the brunt of the attack must inevitably fall after the barrage was lifted.

It had cost him an effort to come across, knowing that Diane was still somewhere in Jersey, and that he might never again be able to cross over and look for her. But in a crisis like this his place was where the greatest danger lay.

Now he was studying the lower bay through a pair of field glasses, trying to pierce the fog of a thick smoke-screen which was being laid down by a squadron of light-draft Purple Navy tenders.

Shells were whining about the building. It had been struck five or six times already, but the stout steel structure did not crumble, even though the masonry was falling from it by the ton. But Jimmy Christopher was oblivious to everything but the vague outline of a ship which showed every now and then through a flurry in the smoke-screen.

Hank Sheridan stepped up beside him. "What do you see, Jimmy?"

Operator 5 handed him the glasses. "I'm sure there's a destroyer making its way past Ellis Island. There are half a dozen tugs around it, taking soundings as they proceed. If a couple of our shore batteries were in commission, we could stop that ship by hitting the tugs. But we haven't got a gun that'll shoot. The barrage crippled us."

OPERATOR 5

THE SIEGE THAT BROUGHT THE BLACK DEATH

Out of the cage, swarming ashore, came the wretched bearers of the Black Plague!

He had to talk very loud to make himself heard, and Hank Sheridan cupped an ear to listen.

General Ferrara strode up to them. There was a frown across his forehead. "If they're getting the soundings of the bay," he said, "I can't understand why the whole fleet doesn't sail in, instead of just one ship. They can't hope to take the city with a single destroyer!"

"I'm afraid," Jimmy Christopher said, very low-voiced, "that they don't want to take the city—yet. I'm afraid this is the actual working out of Colonel Salsoun's plan!"

HE SWUNG away from, crossed the room to a corner where Daisy Gait sat dejectedly. She looked up at him when he approached, but did not speak. She was shivering, as if with ague. The constant cannonading had shattered her nerves. She tried to smile feebly, but was not very successful.

Jimmy looked down at her in kindly fashion. "Look here, Daisy, will you repeat what you know of Salsoun's plan? I remember distinctly that you started to warn your grandfather, back there in the Empire Restaurant. You said something about their intention to *release* something."

He paused, bent low over her. "Come. Can't you think what was the word they used?"

Her lips quivered, and she sobbed. "I wish to God I could, Operator 5. I heard Salsoun talking to Baron Flexner yesterday morning, as I served them, but they were talking in the language of the Purple Empire. All I understood was that they were going to release something. Then the word that followed

THE SIEGE THAT BROUGHT THE BLACK DEATH

was one which I didn't understand—and I can't think of it to save my life."

Jimmy Christopher turned away. He said, "All right, Daisy, you've done your best. Now go and get yourself some rest—if you can, with that damnable bombardment dinning in your ears. Ask one of the boys outside to take you to a bomb-proof cellar."

When Daisy had gone, the staff officers glanced at each other uneasily. Twenty minutes passed. One of them swore softly. "If only they'd land from that destroyer and have it over with! It would be better than sitting here and guessing what they—"

Suddenly, his voice sounded loud in the room—loud and startling. He broke off, flushing. They all realized what had happened. The bombardment had ceased. It was quiet outside.

At once, Jimmy Christopher sprang to the window, lifted his glasses.

"The destroyer is at the dock! There are two queer boxes on the deck—each as big as a small house. They're running out gangplanks." He swung to the others in the room, and they saw that his face had gone white. "I—know what the plan is—now. But it's too late to do anything about it. They held the barrage until the last minute!"

The officers thronged about him, but he wouldn't explain. Frantically he summoned an orderly, rapped out, "Stewart! Semaphore to the men in the pill-boxes at the Battery where that ship is landing. Tell them to open up steady machine-gun fire on that destroyer. They're to try to keep them from landing—*anybody*. And above all, *they're not to engage in hand-to-hand conflict with anyone coming off that ship!*"

OPERATOR 5

Stewart looked puzzled, but he hurried out to obey under the urgent voice of Operator 5. Hank Sheridan stared at Jimmy with dismay. "Jimmy! You think—"

Operator 5 nodded somberly. "If it's what I think it is, then our only hope is that our boys down there obey my order *to the letter*—"

He was looking through his glasses, and groaned. "Too late! They didn't get that semaphore!"

Sheridan and Ferrara, and the others all crowded around the windows, peering through their glasses at the scene unfolding down at the Battery.

A COMPANY of American infantry had deployed out into the open to oppose the landing party which would descend from the ship. At the same time, other Americans took positions at various vantage points from which they could cover the gangplanks.

But no troops appeared on the decks of the destroyer. Instead, the doors of the two huge cages on the foredeck slid open automatically, and a ghastly crowd of ragged men came pelting out from behind the bars, where they had evidently been kept prisoners.

From the bridge of the destroyer, several Purple Empire seamen turned three hoses upon those ragged men. Jimmy could see the steam coming from the water as it spurted out of the nozzles, and as it hit the deck of the ship at the feet of the released prisoners.

It was scalding water!

And those ragged men ran wildly from the burning hot

THE SIEGE THAT BROUGHT THE BLACK DEATH

streams of water—ran toward the gangplank, and down it to the dock with all the speed of fear. Jimmy, peering at them closely, said to those behind him, "Those prisoners are East Indians. They're swarthy and bearded—and diseased!"

The American riflemen, seeing that only a rabble of fear-crazed prisoners was coming down the gangplank, held their fire, and advanced to meet them at bayonet point.

The rabble didn't pause, but spread out, evading the bayonets and running helter-skelter into the streets of the city. The American riflemen refrained from using their bayonets on the poor wretches, and grabbed at them, trying to halt them.

And suddenly, Jimmy saw the Americans shrink away from those poor wretches, let them go. He groaned aloud. The others in the room, realizing at last what was happening, were strangely, fearfully silent.

They watched, helpless to stop it, while the very last of those wretches left the ship and disappeared into the city's streets. And now the riflemen down there made no attempt to stop them—in fact, seemed more afraid of the dirty wretches than of a leaden barrage.

A signalman among them raised his semaphore flags, wagged a message back to headquarters. Jimmy Christopher, watching the man with narrowed eyes, translated it for the others in the room as it came in. It consisted of only two words.

Those words said—

BLACK PLAGUE. BLACK PLAGUE.

The enemy had driven three hundred victims of the Black

Plague into the streets of New York. And now, with its work done, the destroyer moved away from the dock, towed by the tugs, and steamed away down the harbor—leaving the Black Plague to spread in New York!

CHAPTER 10
PERIL OF THE PLAGUE

IN SPITE of the fact that there was no telephone in New York City—no newspapers or town criers—the news spread by word of mouth throughout the city, of the new calamity that threatened.

Somehow, tidings of ill omen are communicated more swiftly than any other kind. Before long, men and women in bomb-proof cellars, and riflemen in dugouts, were talking with their heads close together, eyes grave, lips trembling.

People who had faced privation and cold, torture and rapine, death in defense of their country, now blanched at the thought of the Black Plague. The ravages of that dread disease in the eastern hemisphere had decimated the population of Europe and Asia during the last five years. Whole cities had perished under its putrescent scourge; battles had been lost by both sides because entire armies had fallen victim to the plague.

Bodies rotted in every street in every city from Singapore to Saigon and men feared to remove them—even to touch them. But the hideous disease had about run its course in Europe. Throughout the Purple Invasion one great unspoken dread in

THE SIEGE THAT BROUGHT THE BLACK DEATH

the minds of America's leaders had been lest the plague spread to America.

But the Purple emperor feared it no less than anyone else. Hitherto, he had been careful to prevent its spread by accepting no one for military service who was not thoroughly examined to be sure he bore no taint of the plague. People recalled the time, not so long ago, when the emperor had ordered a troop ship, with its entire human cargo sunk in mid-ocean because a case of Black Plague was discovered aboard it. The Purple Navy had taken care of that. The great guns of the *Rudolph*, the flagship of the navy, had thundered death, and sent the unfortunate troopship to the bottom, regardless of the frantic pleas for mercy from those on board not suffering from the plague.

And now men and women in New York told each other, the emperor had forgotten all that, and had deliberately released three hundred plague-stricken victims upon a city which he hoped to occupy. They couldn't understand it. How could the Emperor Rudolph profit by such action? For even if he destroyed the population, civilian and military, his troops would then be exposed to the plague if they entered to occupy the city.

In the meantime those three hundred wretches roamed the city, desperate and friendless and starving. They sought food, only to find that all supplies were under military regulation, and that they would have to apply at one of the various cantonments in the city to secure rations. People shied away from them, and even the military police feared to touch them, to breathe the same air that they breathed.

OPERATOR 5

THE SIEGE THAT BROUGHT THE BLACK DEATH

PRESIDENT HANK SHERIDAN

DIANE

JOHN GALT

OPERATOR 5

At American G.H.Q., Operator 5 and Hank Sheridan and General Ferrara were discussing the situation.

"There's only one thing to do," Jimmy Christopher told them. "We've got to call for volunteer patrols, each to consist of four or five military police, a doctor and a couple of male nurses. Those patrols will have to scour the town, and pick up every one of those three hundred East Indians. We'll have to intern them somewhere. We must act at once, or the plague will sweep through the city.

A call was issued for volunteers, but there were fewer responses than there would have been to a call for some suicidal military undertaking. At last, however, ten such patrols were organized and sent out into the streets.

But by that time the damage had been done. Somehow, whether through polluted water, or through breathing the same air that those wretches breathed, eighteen civilians were reported as stricken by the Black Plague. That evening there were two hundred and forty cases.

The epidemic was in full sway.

By the following morning it was entirely out of hand. The bodies of many of the original three hundred were found in the streets, dead and bloated. Almost a thousand civilians and American troopers were stricken.

Sanitary facilities were strained to the utmost. There were only two hospitals in operation in New York, and these two could not dare to accept a plague patient, with their wards full as it was, with wounded men and the ordinary sick of a beleaguered city.

THE SIEGE THAT BROUGHT THE BLACK DEATH

The morale of the population was fast slipping, and Operator 5 realized grimly that Rudolph had accomplished, in one single stroke, what all his armies, tanks and huge guns had not been able to accomplish in two years of unremitting, bloody warfare.

Americans had always been a comparatively healthy, virile species of mankind. American businessmen had often been entirely incapacitated from work by a slight headache or a cold—for the very reason that they were ordinarily so healthy, and were not used to sickness. Disease and illness had always been a bogey of Americans, as is evidenced by the great number of accident and health policies sold in the United States before the Purple Invasion.

And now a more dreadful disease than any that had ever afflicted America was flaming across the city. After the years of battle and suffering to preserve their homes, no wonder that it took only this to shatter the spirit of America. Thousands upon thousands of families began an exodus from the city, using the ferry accommodations across the East River to take them out into Long Island where they hoped to escape the plague.

Operator 5 did everything he could to aid those who fled—with one proviso, that everyone who left Manhattan Island must first submit to a test to ascertain whether he carried any plague bacillus. None who was in the least way tainted was permitted to leave Manhattan. In this way, it was hoped to isolate the disease.

Border patrols were established in the northern reaches of Manhattan, and every person attempting to go north into Westchester or Connecticut was stopped and required to show a medical inspection pass.

OPERATOR 5

Through all this, the Purple Navy rode the high seas complacently outside the bay, waiting patiently for the Black Plague to do the work it had not been able to do.

HANK SHERIDAN, pacing up and down at G.H.Q., rubbed a moist hand over his eyes. "I can't understand it," he said to Jimmy Christopher. "What is that fleet waiting for? Surely they don't expect to come in and occupy New York after we're all dead! It would be suicide on their part!"

It was at this point that a breathless orderly entered with a message. "This was relayed by semaphore from Westchester, sir," he said.

The message was from the colonel in charge of the border patrols there. It read—

MONGOL ARMY OF SHAN HI MUNG SOUTH OF WHITE PLAINS. THEY ARE ADVANCING IN FORCE AND DRIVING BACK OUR OUTPOSTS. SHALL I RESIST OR RETREAT?

Jimmy read the message over Sheridan's shoulder, and suddenly snapped his fingers. "I see it now, Hank. Rudolph doesn't intend to occupy New York at all! You know that he promised America to Shan Hi Mung. Well, he's keeping his promise. He's going to let Shan Hi Mung have it. He intends to let Shan Hi Mung become the ruler of a country devastated by the plague!"

Hank Sheridan's eyes widened. "What a devilish thing to do! The Mongol general took him prisoner, and forced him to

THE SIEGE THAT BROUGHT THE BLACK DEATH

promise him America. Rudolph is giving it to him—but not the way he expects it!"

Jimmy nodded. "I know also, why Rudolph hasn't left for Europe yet. He's hanging around on the off chance that he'll capture me before he goes. I guess if he could get me in his power, he'd die happy!"

Hank Sheridan stared out of the window for a long time. "And all of America must suffer, a thousand times worse than it has already suffered, because of the petty spite of a revengeful man! I think—" he said the next words slowly—*"that some one should execute Emperor Rudolph before he leaves the shores of America!"*

For a moment, there was silence in the room. Then Jimmy Christopher's eyes met those of President Sheridan, and there was a terrible resolve in them. He said, very slowly, *"I will undertake that mission, Hank!"*

Hank Sheridan said nothing at all in reply to Operator 5's statement. The silence which Jimmy Christopher had broken to say those six words grew thickly in the room like a pall of dire prophecy.

There was little need of further speech or explanation between these two men. They knew each other too well to require explanation of motives or analysis of feelings. Both were men of action who had seen perilous days and had spent dangerous times together. Both knew that such an undertaking could only mean the death of Operator 5—whether he succeeded or failed. For it was unthinkable that anyone could make an attempt upon the life of the Emperor of the Purple Empire, and escape from the numerous guards who always surrounded him.

By appointing himself the executioner of Rudolph I, Operator 5 was at the same time signing his own death warrant. Yet Hank Sheridan, who loved him as a father would a son, said nothing to dissuade him. In the mind of the Provisional President of the United States, there was the thought that it might be a good thing to die. Today, he saw no hope for America. Against men and guns and war machines he could fight bravely to the end, and die smiling. But against the dread, invisible enemy of the Black Plague he could not fight.

America was in no condition to combat a pestilence. In the two years of the Purple Invasion, our medical and sanitation facilities had been utterly destroyed. Great institutions that might formerly have been capable of coping with the disease, capable of immunizing the population against it and of segregating it scientifically—were no longer in existence. We were a primitive people, fighting disease in a primitive way.

Formerly, our colleges had turned out a surplus of physicians; now, there were no new colleges, and no new students of medicine. For every doctor that was killed or captured by the enemy, there was no one to take his place.

And the plague was spreading.

So Hank Sheridan, who had once been a small-town mayor, and who had risen to be Provisional President of the United States of America, thought that it might be good to die. He envied Operator 5 the idea of dying in such a way as to avenge all of America upon the one man who had caused her misery.

THE SIEGE THAT BROUGHT THE BLACK DEATH

Wearily, he picked up the message from the border. "What'll I do about this, Jimmy? Do we resist Shan Hi Mung—or do we allow his armies to occupy New York?"

Jimmy Christopher shook his head. "We must resist. We must resist as long as there is a chance that the Black Plague can be confined to Manhattan Island. If the Mongol troops of Shan Hi Mung once occupy New York, then they will unwittingly spread the plague to every city and town in the country. Therefore, we must keep them out."

Hank Sheridan nodded. "I'll order them to fight every inch of ground. I'll send all troops not tainted with the plague up into Westchester, and I'll order General Squier to march his ninth route army over here from Connecticut. If Rudolph and his navy are out of the battle we may have a chance to hold Shan Hi Mung."

He sat down and wrote his orders, handed them to the orderly who answered his call. "That's that!" he sighed. "And now, Jimmy—how do you propose to carry out your plan?"

"I'll take along the same men who went in the launch with me," Operator 5 told him. "They're good men, and I think every one of them will be glad of the opportunity. There's a fog over the bay, and we can cross over under cover of the mist and land somewhere opposite Bedloe's Island on the Jersey Shore. Then we can work our way up to Jersey City. For the rest—it's in the laps of the gods!"

CHAPTER 11
DUNGEON OF DOOM

REGAINING CONSCIOUSNESS, Diane Elliot opened her eyes in utter darkness. Her head was whirling, and there was a dull throbbing in her side. At first, her mind was a blank. She felt a great lassitude and did not want to think. She had no idea of where she was or of what had happened to her. She recalled having made her way to the ferry boat with Tim Donovan and of having said good-by to the lad.

Then she remembered that she had begun to grow hot and cold by turns, and that her side had pained dreadfully. She had a hazy recollection of having suffered the tortures of hell while she lay there on the ferry-boat bench and then of having gotten up and staggered out on to the deck.

After that, she remembered nothing.

Now she could not tell where she was, except that she was lying on a cot or a stretcher of some sort, and that it was so dark that she could not see her hand before her face.

Dizzily she swung her legs off the cot, and her bare feet touched cold stone floor.

She found that she was wearing a dress of some sort, but no shoes or stockings. There was a neat bandage along her right side—a bandage that could have been made by none but a practiced physician or nurse.

Now she felt a little stronger, so she attempted to get to her feet. She took two steps and felt dizzy. She thrust out her hand for support, and encountered a cold stone wall. She shuddered.

THE SIEGE THAT BROUGHT THE BLACK DEATH

Her eyes, growing more and more accustomed to the blackness, were now able to distinguish the four walls of a cell. It was a narrow cell, and there was no window—but one wall was broken by a barred door.

Suddenly a cold chill crept through her. There was only one person in the world who would place her in such a dungeon—Rudolph I. She must therefore have wandered off the ferry boat in delirium and been apprehended by the hussars of the Purple Empire.

She started back to her cot and stumbled. The cot scraped against the floor, and the little noise it made sounded tremendous in this secluded dungeon.

Almost at once there came another sound, from somewhere behind her, *"P-s-st!"*

She paused, standing motionless, frozen by the suddenness of the sound. It was repeated almost at once, and she sighed, relieved. Someone was calling to her, repeating it again and again, *"P-s-st!"*

Slowly, she groped her way back to the barred door. The sound came from out there in the corridor. There was someone out there in the darkness.

She gripped the bars, steadied herself, and said, "Yes?"

At once, a man's voice answered her. "Thank God you're conscious at last! I have been calling to you for hours! You are the Elliot girl, are you not—Operator 5's fiancée?"

"Who are you?" she asked, instantly suspicious.

"I am one who was formerly your enemy, but is now your friend. I am to be executed with you in the morning. I think it must be morning now. One cannot tell here, for daylight never enters. I know. I have consigned many men and women to these dungeons in my day. Many have gone mad here."

Diane gripped the bars till her fingers ached. "Who—who are you?"

"I am Colonel Pretorius Salsoun—the man who hunted you in Hoboken yesterday, and who today shares your imprisonment!"

SALSOUN'S VOICE was bitter. She could sense that bitterness, and she knew that he was not lying, was not placed there as a spy to worm information from her. She could understand the colonel's swift reversion of fortune. It had happened to many a brilliant luminary at the court of Rudolph I.

"Tell me quickly," she said. "What has happened since. Was it yesterday that I was caught?"

"Yes. The Americans have attacked and taken Hoboken, led by Operator 5, who came there searching for you. But you had already been caught by Baron Flexner's personal patrols. For my failure to carry out a certain plan, I have been sentenced to death. You and I are both scheduled to die in the morning—very terribly."

Diane felt her way slowly back to the cot. She had expected that, sooner or later, death would come to her in her perilous life. But she had hoped that it would come in the heat of a fight—preferably, when she stood side by side and shoulder to shoulder with Operator 5. But that was not to be. She was to die here, a prisoner of the emperor—to die in some horrible, fiendish fashion while Rudolph and his courtiers looked on, mildly amused.

THE SIEGE THAT BROUGHT THE BLACK DEATH

Into her reverie, Salsoun's eager voice came once more. "Listen. There is still one small chance for us. Would you like to try it?" Then there was silence.

She tautened. Was this some trap of the wily Salsoun's, or of the emperor's? Some hideous joke that would raise her hopes at the last moment, only to extinguish them hopelessly?

She asked carefully, "What do you mean?"

"Are your hands tied?"

"No. They must have thought me too weak from my wound to try to escape."

"Good!" he said. "My hands are bound behind my back with a rawhide thong that I cannot loosen. But listen—they forgot to take my revolver from me. I have gotten it out of my pocket, and it is on the floor. Only I cannot use it. I will kick it over to you. There is a space between the bottom bars and the floor, through which the gun can slide. Use it on the jailer when he comes with the bread and water."

Diane felt a strange thrill course through her. Of course, escape from the jail building would be impossible. But here was a chance to go down fighting.

"All right," she said, trying to hide the eagerness in her voice. "But for God's sake, try to kick straight. Don't miss my door."

"It will not be difficult. My cell is directly opposite yours. Only first you must promise me that you will stop to release me before escaping."

"I promise," she agreed. "But how can we get out of the building?"

"As to that, I cannot tell you. We are in an old office building, which Rudolph has converted into his headquarters. There are other buildings on the block, and perhaps we can find a cellar connection. There is little hope, but anything is worth trying."

"Yes, yes!" Diane exclaimed. "Anything. The gun—kick it over."

"You will remember your promise to release me?"

"Yes."

There was the sound of movement from the opposite cell. She heard a metallic object being shoved carefully into place.

She was in agony of apprehension now, lest Salsoun misgauge his kick, and send the gun out of her reach.

"Careful!" she called urgently.

She heard the impact of the kick, then the sliding scrape of the gun. She was down on her knees now, watching the open space under the bars. Just a little deflection, and it would be out of her reach!

She heard a thud, and could tell that the gun had come to rest. But she couldn't see it. It wasn't there! It had gone wide!

Salsoun called to her, "Have you got it?"

"No!" The word was a whole symphony of agony in itself. "I think it's too far—"

She broke off, gasping with relief. Her frantically groping hand, stretching out through the bars, had encountered the encouraging feel of a gun butt, resting just around the edge of the jamb. Her fingers closed eagerly on it. "I've got it!"

Swiftly, she broke it to make sure it was loaded. Salsoun called out to her in a hoarse whisper, "Now is the time. Here comes the turnkey. Let us pray he is alone!"

THE SIEGE THAT BROUGHT THE BLACK DEATH

SIXTEEN MEN disembarked silently from a motor launch that was drawn in under the shelter of a small cove on the Jersey shore, almost directly opposite Bedloe's Island. All were attired in the peajacket uniforms of Purple seamen, except for the last man to leave the boat, who was in the uniform of a Purple Navy officer. This last man paused for a moment and stared out to sea, where were visible the riding-lights of a hundred great ships of war, comprising the huge fleet of the Purple Empire.

There seemed to be a great deal of activity aboard the fleet this morning. Navy tenders were putting out from spots all along the shore, deeply laden with stores of food and supplies of war. They were being loaded on board the various ships, and going back for further loads. A little less than a quarter of a mile inland, long lines of loaded motor trucks were winding their way south to meet the tenders with more supplies, while empty trucks were returning to Jersey City.

One of the seamen said, "It looks like Rudolph is getting ready to pull out, doesn't it, Operator 5?"

"I'm afraid that's what he's doing, Drummond. I hope he hasn't left with his retinue."

OPERATOR 5

Drummond grinned crookedly. "We'll follow him, if he has!"

The sixteen men now made their way more or less openly to the shore road. Operator 5 lowered his voice. "Look lively now, boys. This'll be a ticklish spot. If anyone connects us with the Hoboken raiders, we'll have to fight our way out of it!"

They reached the road, and stood there for several minutes, without attempting concealment, watching the rolling trucks go by, and sizing up the lay of the land.

At last Operator 5 spotted an empty truck moving toward Jersey City with only a single man in the cab. "All right, boys," he whispered. "We'll tackle this one!"

He raised a commanding hand in signal to halt, and the trooper at the wheel obediently slowed down, came to a stop abreast of him.

"My detail must get to Jersey City urgently," Operator 5 told the driver. "You will carry us there."

He watched the Purple driver like a hawk, for the least sign of suspicion. But the man did not suspect that this naval officer and his detail might be the same that had touched off the battle of Hoboken. He saluted respectfully, and waited while the seamen climbed into the body of the truck, and Operator 5 got in beside him.

The ride to Jersey City took less than twenty minutes, and the truck deposited them in the square in front of the great building where Rudolph made his headquarters. They stared up for a moment at the emblem of the severed head and the crossed broadswords on the flag which flew above the building, then, squaring their shoulders, marched after Jimmy Christopher,

THE SIEGE THAT BROUGHT THE BLACK DEATH

directly into the building! Aides-de-camp, orderlies, messengers and high ranking officers were bustling all about them as they made their way through the lobby. But no one paid them any particular attention. Yet each of the seamen had a hand close to his jacket, where an army issue revolver rested, easy to draw.

Jimmy Christopher knew, from conversing with prisoners taken in the Battle of Hoboken, that the gorgeous throne-room of Rudolph I was on the first floor, and he made his way directly to the staircase.

HIS MEN mounted stiffly behind him, appearing to be nothing but the perfect automata which Purple discipline had made of the military and naval personnel. Yet each one of those fifteen men was keenly alert to everything that went on about them, missing nothing.

At the upper landing, a junior officer, whose uniform was decorated with a good deal of gold braid, stopped them. He eyed Operator 5's uniform questioningly. "No one is permitted to ascend by this staircase," he said, "unless he has business with the court. I do not recognize you, sir."

Jimmy smiled at him. "I have urgent business with the emperor," he said softly. "Kindly take me to him at once."

He accompanied the words with a swift motion that produced the revolver from his holster. At the same time, his detail moved around in such fashion that nothing was visible to the numerous other people hurrying about on the floor.

The junior officer's eyes—widened at sight of the gun. He gasped. "You *dare*—"

Jimmy Christopher's eyes were glittering coldly. "I am Operator 5," he told the other. "You have heard enough about me to know that I always keep my word. I now promise to give you a bullet through the stomach unless you conduct me to the emperor at once."

The Purple subaltern grew white. He saw the cold purpose in Jimmy Christopher's eyes, and heard the irrevocable finality in his voice. He was young, and did not want to die. He gulped. "I—I dare not. I would be drawn and quartered—"

Jimmy Christopher only smiled tightly. "I am going to press the trigger now—"

"Wait! No, don't shoot. I—I'll take you. But not these men. They would not be permitted to enter—"

"Just show me to the emperor's door. We will arrange everything else."

The subaltern turned around as if he had been a puppet propelled by strings held by an invisible master. His knees were shaking, but he managed to walk, with Operator 5 close at his side, and the double column of seamen on either side of them.

Those in the hall glanced at them curiously but they saw the subaltern, and recognized him as one of the emperor's aides, so they gave it no further thought. It was not healthy in court, to investigate too closely into the goings and comings of people.

They reached the huge double doors of the throne-room, and the subaltern halted, wetting his lips. A grenadier stood guard at either side of the door, and all the junior officer had to do was to utter one little word of warning. Jimmy sensed his thoughts, and gripped his arm tightly, pressing the muzzle of the revolver against his side, just beneath the bottom rib.

THE SIEGE THAT BROUGHT THE BLACK DEATH

The grenadiers stared blankly at the detail of men, with the subaltern in the center. But that subaltern's very presence allayed their suspicions for the crucial moment that it took the bogus seamen to handle them. As if by prearranged plan, three of the seamen took each grenadier. Suddenly, guns appeared in their hands, and before the grenadiers could bring their carbines into action, a neat chopping stroke with the muzzle of a gun had disposed of each of them.

But that could not pass without notice. Someone in the hall uttered a shout, and many of the officers turned, reaching for swords or guns. It was then that Lieutenant Drummond pulled the sub-machine gun from under his great coat and knelt upon the floor, covering the entire corridor.

"Let no one move," he ordered, "or I will spray the hall with lead!"

Thunderstruck, the officers in the hall stood immobile, frozen into inaction by the very unbelievable monstrosity of such an attempt in the very headquarters of the emperor.

The teamwork of this small group of men was a thing of synchronic beauty. While six men overpowered the two grenadiers, while Operator 5 held the subaltern under the threat of his revolver, and while Drummond commanded the hall with the sub-machine gun, two other seamen pushed open the double doors of the throne-room, standing aside so that another group of three could step past them into the room.

Each of this last group of three produced a sub-machine gun from under his great coat, and they spread out fanwise so as to cover the entire room, completely.

OPERATOR 5

RUDOLPH I was seated upon his throne. In the small chair near him sat the woman, Mistra, while three or four courtiers hovered around the emperor. Neither Flexner nor Marshal Kremer nor Admiral von der Selz was present.

There was a detail of six grenadiers in the room, the personal bodyguard of the emperor. But under the threat of those sub-machine guns they dropped their rifles without even attempting to fire a shot.

Rudolph half-rose from his seat. Then as one of the seamen swung the sub-machine gun toward him, Rudolph's mouth dropped open and he sank back upon his throne. The woman, Mistra, tautened perceptibly, then relaxed, a faint smile hovering about her lips. She leaned slightly forward so that the V of her black dress fell open at the throat for the seamen to see. Otherwise, she did not move.

Now, Jimmy Christopher, having turned over custody of the subaltern to one of the other men in the hall, stepped into the room.

There was a gasp of recognition from Rudolph. "Operator 5!"

The woman, Mistra, started and her eyes narrowed. She studied the well-knit, athletic figure of Jimmy Christopher with sudden interest.

Jimmy Christopher walked slowly into the room, keeping out of the line of fire of the machine guns. From out in the hall there came the sound of rushing feet, and then the crisp voice of Drummond.

"Stand still, all of you. Your emperor is a prisoner of Operator 5. Do not attempt to defy us, or your emperor may die!"

THE SIEGE THAT BROUGHT THE BLACK DEATH

Rudolph's gaunt face had suddenly become tinged with yellow. He was speechless.

Jimmy Christopher said, "Well, Rudolph, you have been looking for me a long time. Here I am!"

At last, Rudolph found his voice. "What—what do you want?"

Operator 5 waited a moment, glancing about the room. He noted the half-interested, half-amused expression on Mistra's face; noted the frozen fear of the courtiers and the grenadiers. They could not yet believe that this was really an attack upon their emperor, right in the heart of imperial headquarters.

Jimmy Christopher turned from them, and faced the emperor. He said in a voice that was heavy with the weight of doom; "Rudolph, once before you were a captive of the United States of America, and you escaped. But you were tried in your absence by the Second Continental Congress. You were found guilty of mass murder, and of armed attempt against the peace and safety of the United States of America. You were sentenced to death, and that sentence was duly approved by the Provisional President of the United States of America. Now I, Operator 5 of the United States Intelligence service, have come to carry out that sentence upon you. Stand up, Rudolph, and meet your fate!"

He raised his revolver deliberately, slowly, carefully.

Now Rudolph broke down. The Emperor of all of Europe and Asia, the self-styled master of America, the man who dispensed the high justice and the low to tens of millions of human beings—that mighty man broke down and begged for his life.

OPERATOR 5

It was a despicable scene.

"No—no, Operator 5! Don't kill me.

I can give you anything you want. I can give you a thousand—a million slaves. I can make you a prince in Europe or Asia, or even a king. I will give you any thing...."

His voice died away before the implacable coldness in Operator 5's eyes. He gurgled, and a low moan escaped his lips.

Jimmy Christopher leveled his revolver. "Will you take it cringing in your chair, Rudolph, or standing up like a man?" His finger tautened on the trigger. In that instant, he would surely have fired a shot into the heart of Rudolph I, had not Mistra interrupted.

Lazily, moving with the litheness of a well-fed cat, she arose from her chair, moved over to stand in front of the emperor, facing Jimmy Christopher's revolver.

Operator 5, a brave man himself, was never slow to recognize bravery in another. He saw the cruelty in her eyes, the cold merciless set of her lips. He knew that she was one of those human beings who can inflict pain and agony upon others and enjoy it. Yet he had to admit that she was brave.

He stayed his finger upon the trigger.

The woman spoke slowly, distinctly. "Let us make a trade, Operator 5. For the life of the emperor, I will give you the life of one you love very dearly. Diane Elliot is a prisoner of the Empire. The ships are sailing away. She will be left to rot in the place where she is kept, unless she is freed!"

JIMMY CHRISTOPHER felt a tight compression about his chest, like a steel band closing in inexorably. He had known

THE SIEGE THAT BROUGHT THE BLACK DEATH

all along, been sure, that Diane was a prisoner of the enemy. Now it had come up to face him. He fully believed that what Mistra said was true. But could he betray the men who had come along with him risking their lives in this undertaking? Could he let down Hank Sheridan, who was fighting the Mongols now, and praying for Operator 5's success?

It was the life of Diane Elliot against the honor of America, and the honor and lives of these men who had followed him today.

Jimmy's lips formed a thin tight line of agony. "Stand aside!" he said hoarsely.

Mistra raised her eyebrows. "You will sacrifice the woman you love for your silly country? You cannot be much of a man!"

Almost tonelessly, Jimmy Christopher repeated, "Stand aside or I'll shoot through you!"

Behind her, Rudolph was whimpering like a beaten animal. "Don't shoot, Operator 5. Give me five minutes more time, and I'll bring you the Elliot girl. I'll give you—"

His voice was cut off as if by a huge knife slicing through the air. His eyes widened, staring toward the window.

Operator 5 did not take his eyes from Rudolph or from Mistra. But he heard the startled ejaculations of his own men, behind him. They were staring out across the courtyard to the window on the same floor, but in the next wing. Framed in that window were two faces. One of them was that of Diane Elliot; the other was the countenance of Colonel Pretorius Salsoun.

Salsoun was holding his own revolver once more aiming it at Emperor Rudolph, through the open window. His face was a mask of hate, and he did not say a word as he squeezed the trigger, firing three times in quick succession.

All three of his shots took effect in the body of Rudolph. The emperor of the world uttered a piercing shriek of fright and agony, and collapsed to the floor, hugging both hands tight to his stomach.

The woman, Mistra, did not move. Fortunately for her, she had not been in Salsoun's line of fire, for she had been standing directly in front of the emperor. Now she merely stood there staring out across the courtyard with steeled gaze.

Salsoun uttered a great shout of hate. "Die, Rudolph!" he screamed. "Die slowly—you who would have tortured me for a blunder!" Then he turned to face Diane. "And *you!* You are the cause of all my troubles. Die!" He raised the revolver once more.

Diane was pale, wobbly. She had exerted herself too much in the last half hour in aiding Salsoun to escape. Now she tottered, unable to defend herself. In another instant, the colonel would have shot her through the head.

But Operator 5 fired a single shot across the courtyard, and Salsoun's gun fell from nerveless fingers, while a black hole appeared in his temple. His inert body slumped across the windowsill.

Now the whole room was in an uproar. Outside, the courtiers and officers in the hall made a concerted effort to rush the Americans, and Lieutenant Drummond's machine gun began to spit fire. He mowed them down without mercy, sending two quick bursts along the length of the hall. A dozen of them fell under the trip-hammer barrage. The others, instead of taking

THE SIEGE THAT BROUGHT THE BLACK DEATH

cover in doorways along the hall and returning his fire—as any American group of men might have done under the circumstances—turned and ran for dear life!

BY THIS time there was a great uproar outside in the streets, and a company of guards came goose-stepping over from the waterfront. They did not enter the building, as their officers were afraid to brave the emperor's anger. Those officers were between the devil and the deep blue sea, for, if the emperor were in danger they would be shot for failing to aid him; but, if he were not in danger, they would be punished for presuming to enter imperial headquarters without orders.

So, while they hesitated outside, the courtiers came streaming out, running in blind fear of that machine gun upstairs. *"The emperor is dead! The emperor is dead!"*

Meanwhile, upstairs in the throne-room, Jimmy Christopher was at the window, calling to Diane to answer him. She must have fainted from weakness, for her slim form had slid down out of sight beneath the windowsill at the moment when Operator 5 shot Salsoun.

Jimmy peered out of the window and saw that it would be useless for him to attempt to run down to the ground floor, and again up to the first floor of the next wing where Diane lay. There were too many Purple soldiers in the courtyard. He turned back into the room and his glance swept frantically over the furnishings.

His eyes lighted on a tremendously long conference table at the far end of the room. Under his quick, desperate orders, two of his men ripped the cloth-of-gold from the table-top, then

OPERATOR 5

dragged off one of the long boards in the movable top. They hurried with it over to the window, and slid it out toward the window in the opposite wing. It was just long enough to span the courtyard, with not an inch to spare. The slightest push one way or the other would send it hurtling down into the yard below.

But Jimmy Christopher didn't stop to consider the danger. He vaulted out over the windowsill, and fairly ran across the plank, while half a dozen soldiers from the street below, as well as from the upper windows of the building, fired at him.

He reached the other side in safety, leaped to the floor and bent over Diane. He had to push aside the dead body of Salsoun to reach her, and he did so unceremoniously. Then he raised her to his shoulder, slung her across and stepped out once more upon the plank, just as a shout sounded from behind. Several Purple guards were coming up the stairs, and had sighted him.

Shots whined through the air, whistling past his ears. He ran across the plank, and it shook under the combined weight of himself and Diane. At the far window his own men were reaching out eager, willing hands to help him over the last lap.

He was almost there when he heard a triumphant shout from behind him and felt the plank almost jerked out from under his feet. The guards behind, having found guns ineffectual, had thought of sliding the plank that half inch that stood between safety and disaster.

Jimmy fairly leaped across the last two feet of that plank. Half a dozen hands grasped him and Diane, dragging them in through the window just as the plank went toppling down into the yard below.

THE SIEGE THAT BROUGHT THE BLACK DEATH

WITHIN THE room, the echoes of the commotion outside in the street came up in a rolling crescendo of panic and hate, drowning out the feeble moans of Rudolph who lay upon his face on the floor.

Of the woman, Mistra, there was no trace. She had slipped out through some back passage, unobserved.

Drummond, who had turned over his machine gun to one of the other men, had cleared the room of all the courtiers and now he faced Operator 5, grimly.

"The emperor of the world," he said, "is through. He won't live an hour. Salsoun has saved us the trouble of executing him. But how are we going to get out of this—if at all?"

Jimmy Christopher was holding Diane in his arms. His eyes swept the courtyard, and his lips twisted in a smile. "I don't think we need to worry about getting out of here," he said quietly. "They're leaving the place to us. Look—the rats are deserting the sinking ship!"

Drummond uttered a low whistle, and stepped to the window. It was true. Instead of gathering to storm the imperial headquarters, the troops were slowly fading away toward the riverfront where the navy tenders were waiting for them.

Drummond grinned. "That last batch of courtiers that I turned out of here brought the crowd the authentic news that the emperor is really through. They don't want any more of America. It's a good thing the fleet is here to take them home!"

For an hour, that small group of men stood there in what had once been imperial headquarters and watched the steady exodus of Purple troopers.

OPERATOR 5

At last, Jersey City was free of enemy occupation. Great crowds of civilians came into the streets, cheering, dancing.

And far out in the bay the long line of ships of the navy of the Purple Empire sent spirals of smoke into the air as they sailed away for home, leaving the first land which the might of their armies had failed to conquer. They left behind, too, the dead body of a man who had aspired to rule the world by force and torture and hatred, but who had ended by lying, riddled by a retainer's bullets, dead under the eyes of the man he hated most.

Rudolph I, Emperor of the Purple Empire, Master of Europe and Asia, lay dead—unsung, unhonored, and unwept.

And with his gaze toward the east where lay New York City, Operator 5 faced, in his mind's eye, the task of building a new America out of the plague-ridden, devastated country which was his own native land.*

---

* AUTHOR'S NOTE: America was now faced with the prospect of segregating the dreaded Black Plague which Rudolph had spread; of freeing the country of raiding bands of Mongols, of Goths, and of vicious guerrilla warriors of the Purple Armies who spread terror from coast to coast. With all this, she had to build industry, agriculture—in short she had to grow a new civilization upon the ashes of the old. In the course of this task, Operator 5 and Hank Sheridan found themselves faced with a new and greater danger than had ever arisen before. The novel to be published in the forthcoming issue will deal with the days of swift peril and breath-taking risk which followed immediately after the death of Rudolph.

POPULAR HERO PULPS AVAILABLE NOW:

THE SPIDER
- ❏ #1: The Spider Strikes — $13.95
- ❏ #2: The Wheel of Death — $13.95
- ❏ #3: Wings of the Black Death — $13.95
- ❏ #4: City of Flaming Shadows — $13.95
- ❏ #5: Empire of Doom! — $13.95
- ❏ #6: Citadel of Hell — $13.95
- ❏ #7: The Serpent of Destruction — $13.95
- ❏ #8: The Mad Horde — $13.95
- ❏ #9: Satan's Death Blast — $13.95
- ❏ #10: The Corpse Cargo — $13.95
- ❏ #11: Prince of the Red Looters — $13.95
- ❏ #12: Reign of the Silver Terror — $13.95
- ❏ #13: Builders of the Dark Empire — $13.95
- ❏ #14: Death's Crimson Juggernaut — $13.95
- ❏ #15: The Red Death Rain — $13.95
- ❏ #16: The City Destroyer — $13.95
- ❏ #17: The Pain Emperor — $13.95
- ❏ #18: The Flame Master — $13.95
- ❏ #19: Slaves of the Crime Master — $13.95
- ❏ #20: Reign of the Death Fiddler — $13.95
- ❏ #21: Hordes of the Red Butcher — $13.95
- ❏ #22: Dragon Lord of the Underworld — $13.95
- ❏ #23: Master of the Death-Madness — $13.95
- ❏ #24: King of the Red Killers — $13.95
- ❏ #25: Overlord of the Damned — $13.95
- ❏ #26: Death Reign of the Vampire King — $13.95
- ❏ #27: Emperor of the Yellow Death — $13.95
- ❏ #28: The Mayor of Hell — $13.95
- ❏ #29: Slaves of the Murder Syndicate — $13.95
- ❏ #30: Green Globes of Death — $13.95
- ❏ #31: The Cholera King — $13.95
- ❏ #32: Slaves of the Dragon — $13.95
- ❏ #33: Legions of Madness — $12.95
- ❏ #34: Laboratory of the Damned — $12.95
- ❏ #35: Satan's Sightless Legion — $12.95
- ❏ #36: The Coming of the Terror — $12.95
- ❏ #37: The Devil's Death-Dwarfs — $12.95
- ❏ #38: City of Dreadful Night — $12.95
- ❏ #39: Reign of the Snake Men — $12.95
- ❏ #40: Dictator of the Damned — $12.95
- ❏ #41: The Mill-Town Massacres — $12.95
- ❏ #42: Satan's Workshop — $12.95
- ❏ #43: Scourge of the Yellow Fangs — $12.95
- ❏ #44: The Devil's Pawnbroker — $12.95
- ❏ #45: Voyage of the Coffin Ship — $12.95
- ❏ #46: The Man Who Ruled in Hell — $13.95
- ❏ #47: Slaves of the Black Monarch — $13.95
- ❏ #48: Machineguns Over the White House — $13.95
- ❏ #49: The City That Dared Not Eat — $13.95
- ❏ #50: Master of the Flaming Horde — $13.95
- ❏ #51: Satan's Switchboard — $13.95
- ❏ #52: Legions of the Accursed Light — $13.95
- ❏ #53: The City of Lost Men — $13.95
- ❏ #54: The Grey Horde Creeps — $13.95
- ❏ #55: City of Whispering Death — $13.95
- ❏ #56: When Thousands Slept in Hell — $13.95
- ❏ #57: Satan's Shakles — $14.95
- ❏ #58: The Emperor From Hell — $14.95
- ❏ #59: The Devil's Candlesticks — $14.95
- ❏ #60: The City That Paid to Die — $14.95
- ❏ #61: The Spider at Bay — $14.95
- ❏ #62: Scourge of the Black Legions — $14.95
- ❏ #63: The Withering Death — $14.95
- ❏ #64: Claws of the Golden Dragon — $14.95
- ❏ #65: The Song of Death — $14.95
- ❏ #66: The Silver Death Reign — $14.95
- ❏ #67: Blight of the Blazing Eye — $14.95
- ❏ #68: King of the Fleshless Legion — $14.95
- ❏ *NEW:* #69: Rule of the Monster Men — $16.95

THE WESTERN RAIDER
- ❏ #1: Guns of the Damned — $13.95
- ❏ #2: The Hawk Rides Back from Death — $13.95
- ❏ #3: Gun-Call for the Lost Legion — $13.95
- ❏ #4: The Law of Silver Trent — $13.95
- ❏ #5: The Gun-Prayer of Silver Trent — $13.95
- ❏ #6: Silver Trent Rides Alone — $13.95

G-8 AND HIS BATTLE ACES
- ❏ #1: The Bat Staffel — $13.95

CAPTAIN SATAN
- ❏ #1: The Mask of the Damned — $13.95
- ❏ #2: Parole for the Dead — $13.95
- ❏ #3: The Dead Man Express — $13.95
- ❏ #4: A Ghost Rides the Dawn — $13.95
- ❏ #5: The Ambassador From Hell — $13.95

DR. YEN SIN
- ❏ #1: Mystery of the Dragon's Shadow — $12.95
- ❏ #2: Mystery of the Golden Skull — $12.95
- ❏ #3: Mystery of the Singing Mummies — $12.95

RED FINGER
- ❏ *NEW:* #1: Second-Hand Death — $24.95

POPULAR HERO PULPS AVAILABLE NOW:

ACE G-MAN
- ❏ #1: The Suicide Squad Reports for Death $14.95
- ❏ #2: Coffins for the Suicide Squad $14.95
- ❏ #3: Shells for the Suicide Squad $14.95
- ❏ #4: The Suicide Squad in Corpse-Town $14.95
- ❏ #5: Wanted–In Three Pine Coffins $14.95
- ❏ #6: The Suicide Squad's Dawn Patrol $14.95

OPERATOR 5
- ❏ #1: The Masked Invasion $13.95
- ❏ #2: The Invisible Empire $13.95
- ❏ #3: The Yellow Scourge $13.95
- ❏ #4: The Melting Death $13.95
- ❏ #5: Cavern of the Damned $13.95
- ❏ #6: Master of Broken Men $13.95
- ❏ #7: Invasion of the Dark Legions $13.95
- ❏ #8: The Green Death Mists $13.95
- ❏ #9: Legions of Starvation $13.95
- ❏ #10: The Red Invader $13.95
- ❏ #11: The League of War-Monsters $13.95
- ❏ #12: The Army of the Dead $13.95
- ❏ #13: March of the Flame Marauders $13.95
- ❏ #14: Blood Reign of the Dictator $13.95
- ❏ #15: Invasion of the Yellow Warlords $13.95
- ❏ #16: Legions of the Death Master $13.95
- ❏ #17: Hosts of the Flaming Death $13.95
- ❏ #18: Invasion of the Crimson Death Cult $13.95
- ❏ #19: Attack of the Blizzard Men $13.95
- ❏ #20: Scourge of the Invisible Death $13.95
- ❏ #21: Raiders of the Red Death $13.95
- ❏ #22: War-Dogs of the Green Destroyer $13.95
- ❏ #23: Rockets From Hell $13.95
- ❏ #24: War-Masters from the Orient $13.95
- ❏ #25: Crime's Reign of Terror $13.95
- ❏ #26: Death's Ragged Army $13.95
- ❏ #27: Patriots' Death Battalion $13.95
- ❏ #28: The Bloody Forty-five Days $13.95
- ❏ #29: America's Plague Battalions $13.95
- ❏ #30: Liberty's Suicide Legions $13.95
- ❏ #31: Siege of the Thousand Patriots $13.95
- ❏ #32: Patriots' Death March $14.95
- ❏ #33: Revolt of the Lost Legions $14.95
- ❏ #34: Drums of Destruction $14.95
- ❏ #35: The Army Without a Country $14.95
- ❏ #36: The Bloody Frontiers $14.95
- ❏ #37: The Coming of the Mongol Hordes $14.95
- ❏ **NEW:** #38: The Siege That Brought the Black Death $16.95

CAPTAIN COMBAT
- ❏ #1: The Sky Beast of Berlin $13.95
- ❏ #2: Red Wings For the Blood Battalion $13.95
- ❏ #3: Low Ceiling For Nazi Hell Hawks $13.95

DUSTY AYRES AND HIS BATTLE BIRDS
- ❏ #1: Black Lightning! $13.95
- ❏ #2: Crimson Doom $13.95
- ❏ #3: The Purple Tornado $13.95
- ❏ #4: The Screaming Eye $13.95
- ❏ #5: The Green Thunderbolt $13.95
- ❏ #6: The Red Destroyer $13.95
- ❏ #7: The White Death $13.95
- ❏ #8: The Black Avenger $13.95
- ❏ #9: The Silver Typhoon $13.95
- ❏ #10: The Troposphere F-S $13.95
- ❏ #11: The Blue Cyclone $13.95
- ❏ #12: The Tesla Raiders $13.95

MAVERICKS
- ❏ #1: Five Against the Law $12.95
- ❏ #2: Mesquite Manhunters $12.95
- ❏ #3: Bait for the Lobo Pack $12.95
- ❏ #4: Doc Grimson's Outlaw Posse $12.95
- ❏ #5: Charlie Parr's Gunsmoke Cure $12.95

THE MYSTERIOUS WU FANG
- ❏ #1: The Case of the Six Coffins $12.95
- ❏ #2: The Case of the Scarlet Feather $12.95
- ❏ #3: The Case of the Yellow Mask $12.95
- ❏ #4: The Case of the Suicide Tomb $12.95
- ❏ #5: The Case of the Green Death $12.95
- ❏ #6: The Case of the Black Lotus $12.95
- ❏ #7: The Case of the Hidden Scourge $12.95

THE SECRET 6
- ❏ #1: The Red Shadow $13.95
- ❏ #2: House of Walking Corpses $13.95
- ❏ #3: The Monster Murders $13.95
- ❏ #4: The Golden Alligator $13.95

CAPTAIN ZERO
- ❏ #1: City of Deadly Sleep $13.95
- ❏ #2: The Mark of Zero! $13.95
- ❏ #3: The Golden Murder Syndicate $13.95